The Rose Diary

C MAYNARD
LIL BARCASKI

ACKNOWLEDGEMENTS

A special thank you to so many friends and family. My wife Pamela. Nathan and my friends at Gulf Coast Hobby. My film friends. Too many to individually list.

To my son Bentley. As you grow and learn the ways of the world, always keep your head up in the valleys. Then you'll fly high on the mountains.

To my co-writer Lil, thank you for your amazing work. You have such talent and leadership.

Curtis Maynard

Chapter 1

I was only eight years old when the fire happened.

Mrs. Brown, our next-door neighbor, lost her first-born son in that terrible accident. Chace, just 16 years old, had gone to a friend's house to spend the weekend, just a typical high school gathering. The kids that escaped said it was just the usual, a bunch of teens hanging out, spending a Saturday night together, watching horror movies, eating junk food. They heard a really loud boom like something blew, and the next thing they knew there were flames everywhere. Most of them escaped by climbing up and out the basement window before the fire made it downstairs, but Chace and two of his friends had gone up to get more snacks and sodas. They were in the kitchen near the boiler that blew and were in the thick of it. Two of them sustained serious injuries and were in critical condition for several days. They were able to explain the horror they'd experienced when they recovered. Chace was not as lucky and died in the ambulance on the way to the hospital. When I heard of his death, all I could think about was how much I'd miss Chace and his big bear hugs. He was a big kid, man-sized and strong, and sometimes he would finish the hug by throwing me in the air, my chubby little body feeling weightless like I was made of clouds. The best thing was, I knew he would always catch me. He was always kind to me. I knew I would forever miss the handfuls of candy he would dump into my trick or treat sack on Halloween. He spoiled me and I missed him like crazy.

It was rainy and gloomy on the day of Chace's funeral. The weather in our little gulf town of Fairhope, Alabama seemed determined to match the mood of this terrible occasion. I hated black, but I wore a frilly black dress that my mother had forced me to put on. I was fuming, and I took Barbara, my most prized doll, with me for company. She was my moral support and could always keep me happy.

Chace's eldest sister read his eulogy, but I couldn't focus on her words. My eyes were glued on Mrs. Brown who sat in the front pew crying her heart out, sputtering and coughing. It broke my young heart to see her act like that.

Mrs. Brown had never cried, at least not in front of me, in my entire life. Mrs. Brown was the pretty woman next door whose piano playing would wake me up on Saturday mornings as it drifted out of her living room window. She was the neighbor you could count on for delicious cupcakes she baked on Wednesdays. I sat still and watched her take a hanky, mopping her tear-stained cheeks continuously. After several minutes, I couldn't take it anymore and rose from my seat.

"Where are you going?" My mother said in her loudest whisper.

"Mrs. Brown needs me," I replied flatly as I patted down the annoying frills of my dress and marched down the center aisle of the church to sit by Mrs. Brown.

"It's okay, Mrs. Brown," I said. "God is nice. He'll be really nice to Chace up in heaven."

Mrs. Brown kissed my forehead, but I was disappointed when her tears kept pouring forth. After the service, they processed his 'body' to the burial site. When they finally lowered the casket part-way into the deep hole, people formed a line, and as they passed, they tossed a rose down on top of the coffin. When my turn came, I dropped my favorite doll, Barbara, onto his coffin below.

"Here, Chace," I said. "Barbara will keep you company so at least you won't be lonely down there."

I remember crying about how much I would miss her, but I loved Chace very much. It was a huge decision for a young girl of eight to make. My mom told me she was proud of me and that some things had to be sacrificed for love. Then she said we'd shop for another doll, so I stopped crying after a while.

My Dad drove us back home, and I sat in the back seat with my older sister, Sandra, both of us staring out the windows at the trees and buildings that zoomed past, deep in our own world of thoughts. Sandra tapped my knee and I looked her way, waiting for her to speak for what seemed like an eternity. Finally, when she did, she said, "I don't want to die, Jacky. The grave looks like a scary place to be and I'm claustrophobic." I had no idea what she meant. At eight, my vocabulary was still pretty limited, I guess.

Oddly, just days later, I had heard that word again, this time from my mother's lips during a conversation with my father. She was describing how Mrs. Brown felt in her house; claustrophobic and anxious. Not long after that, a moving truck was parked in front of the Browns' family house, and I had to bid the Browns goodbye. They left our lovely suburbs forever because Mrs. Brown felt *claustrophobic*, I guess, though the meaning still escaped me. No more piano music to float to my window accompanied by the envious sonorous singing of Mrs. Brown, and no more delicious cupcakes to look forward to on Wednesday afternoon after school.

Death was truly wicked, and I hated it.

One day, I decided to look up *claustrophobic* in the dictionary. The meaning of that huge word caused me to stammer each time I tried to pronounce it. *Extreme fear of confined places.* But the Brown's house was big, bigger than ours, so why would Mrs. Brown feel claustrophobic? Little did I know that one could feel that way even in the largest of mansions, and four years later, the meaning came to me in the worst possible way. I felt claustrophobic in my own body.

One week after Thanksgiving, death returned to our once-happy little world. This time it came directly to our doorstep. It slipped in uninvited and took silent steps up the staircase, into my sweet sister Sandra's room and snuffed out her life while she slept. It was my mother's screams that woke me when dawn had barely cracked, a hauntingly pain-filled screeching noise that pierced my eardrums. Sandra lay on her bed unmoving, eyes unblinking, staring at the ceiling, her mouth slightly ajar. She looked frightened as if the monster called death had terrified her before snatching her life from her body.

Maybe death possessed supernatural powers, as well, because its visit numbed me, and every other thing that happened after that passed by in an emotionless blur. My mother's screams and cries haunted me, melancholy ringing in each and every wail. My father tried to console her when Sandra's lifeless body was driven off to the mortuary in a van. I felt like I was living in a nightmare, the one you try so hard to wake up from, desperate to escape, but you're stuck in the never-ending loop. Sandra had not been feeling well for weeks, but it seemed like a lingering stomach bug or flu. She complained of nausea and a little dizziness, but Sandra was never the type of person to complain about much. She took some stomach medicine and had seemed fine when I said goodnight to her before bed. Nothing would have made me believe we would wake to find her dead.

As the days flew past and Sandra's absence filled the house with a noisy void, I knew there was no waking up from this nightmarish reality.

Once again, I donned the dreaded color black on the Saturday following Sandra's passing, but this time settled for black leather pants and a black tee shirt, much to my mother's chagrin. This time I was the one sitting in the front pew, a feeling of *déjà vu* washing over me, and the memory of my eight-year-old self was seated close to me. She had no words to comfort me because she knew there were no words on earth that could.

The choir sang a slow, sad hymn, something Sandra would have cringed at. In my mind's eye, I could see her plugging her earpiece in and turning up the volume on her iPod; a Justin Bieber song bleeding into her ears.

My parents asked me to be one to deliver the eulogy. I did my best to find the words, but only gave a short one that lasted a total of a minute and a half. It was bland, no tears, no cracking of voice, not one iota of sadness was reflected in my tone as I recited it. It was like a humongous chore I wanted to get over and done with. Each word suffocated my throat, and the pitiful stares from the congregation made me want to bolt out the door and walk away from all this sadness and sorrow.

Later, at the graveside, as they lowered Sandra's body down into the deep, rich, black earth below, I wondered if Sandra would know what claustrophobia felt like when she was dead. But the dead were called dead for a reason. They didn't have feelings anymore, claustrophobic or otherwise; at least I hoped not, for my sister's sake.

I spent a long time after that doing nothing, at least nothing productive. The house was filled with family members for days, but I stayed in my room for long hours on end avoiding the cacophony beneath my floorboards. Only my Aunt Margaret came up to check up on me or place a meal on my bedside table. Christy, my closest friend, came often; but later I began to lock the door to my room and ignore her gentle knocks to be let in. I didn't know if I should feel guilty about the fact that not a single tear had rolled from my eyes since my sister's death. That little fact had my father very worried.

"Jacky," he knocked gently at my door, slowly pushing it open to slip into my room. "You know you can talk to me. There's no shame in crying. I know you're growing up, but you're still a young girl. She was your sister and I know how much you loved her. You have to let your feelings out."

But how could I cry when I no longer seemed to possess the ability to feel anymore? Numb. All I felt was numb. Every time I tried to move, it felt like I was wading through chest-high snow, every movement a Herculean task.

"At least throw something or break something, "my father told me.

Oddly, the only thing I wanted to break was my mother's jars of pickles in the fridge. I had always hated the nasty taste of pickles since I was little, the slimy consistency and bitter taste traumatizing my taste buds. But even when I opened the fridge to get a glass of milk, I stared at it, unable to even get the momentum up to lift the jar from the shelf. I wanted to. I wanted to grab it and hurl it against the wall, watch the glass shatter as its contents slid gracelessly to the floor, shards of pickle jar and slimy pickle juice mixing into a delightful ooze. I could see it like a movie in my head; but instead, I would pull out the milk container and leave the pickles safe and sound, my rage still intact.

I only spoke when spoken to, said a few words when necessary, and I instantly rejected therapy. The morbid thought of speaking to someone I barely knew who would scribble meaningless words on a notepad, continually pushing me to talk so he or she could get paid, was not an option for me.

Most days, I wondered if death was still lurking around in the corners of the house, or perhaps in the darkness so suited to its personality, watching the consequences of its actions, how it created a crying mother, an overthinking father, and a numb child. I needed any kind of distraction, so when school started a few weeks later, I could not have been more thankful.

Chapter 2

School was a blessing, a haven, a respite from the emptiness in my chest when I was at home. At least, while I was in school, I got to be with my two best friends.

Christabel had been a huge supportive friend all through the depressing time surrounding Sandra's death. Even though all she did was sit in silence with me in my room all day long, her presence was in and of itself comforting.

Sarah, my other bestie, had been traveling in France with her parents when Sandra died, and over and over again, she kept pouring out apologies for not being there with me at the worst time of my life thus far.

"Don't worry," I smiled after she apologized for the hundredth time. "It's not like you could have known my sister was going to die. It's not like ruining your vacation was going to change anything or bring her back. I wouldn't expect you to do that and I wouldn't have done any differently if the shoe were on the other foot. People die no matter where you are."

Sarah listened intently to my retort. She looked at me as if to say that she didn't know if I was being sincere or sarcastic and just kept mute. She had gained a little weight during the school break, I noticed, but she still looked beautiful. Sarah had always been the pretty one, like a human Barbie doll with brains. Christy, short for Christabel, was the nerdy one who replaced her glasses for contacts, and I had been always been Jacqueline; quiet, reserved and calm. Now my personality had intensified to the point where it brought a certain discomfort to the people around me. The color black, which I always detested, had grown on me. I didn't see the change in me, didn't know that I was slowly transitioning into a pseudo-goth kid. My new change of wardrobe irritated my mother to no end, and every morning it was a clash of words. For someone who barely got into fights, I did so almost every day now, the angry frown etched on my face like a permanent, unpleasant feature.

"How are you, Jacqueline?" Christy asked, the bright, almost neon green contacts she was wearing in her eyes were distracting. I wanted to tell her that they made her upsetting to look at and that her natural brown irises suited her far more. She was staring at me with concern, so I tucked my opinions away and nodded silently at her question.

"We should go eat," Sarah suggested, saving me from an awkward moment, linking her arm with mine. "I'm starving."

"Those chocolate soufflés must have been really delicious," Christy said to her.

Sarah immediately stopped walking and turned her head sharply to face Christy, so sharply in fact, I thought her pretty neck would snap.

"And what is that supposed to mean?" She frowned.

"Uh..." Christy looked at me for help. "That I want to taste them? What else would it mean?"

Sarah apparently didn't believe her because, at the lunch table, she kept pushing her fries away and instead nibbled at her baby carrots and drank a ton of water. Christy's comment was clearly an insinuation that she had gained weight, which was her worst nightmare. I ate a little, not having much of an appetite. It was hard to eat with the whispers and pitiful stares surrounding me in the cafeteria. Even though I kept my head bowed, I felt them all.

"Hey, Jacky."

My head shot up instantly. Sadness and disappointment flooded through me when I realized the person calling my name was Caramel, the younger sister of Sandra's best friend, ironically named Sugar. Something felt caught in my throat. I didn't realize that hearing the name 'Jacky' would provoke so many emotions I thought had died inside me. It was Sandra who gave me that nickname. She never called me Jacqueline, always Jacky. For a brief moment, I had thought it was my sister who was calling out for me, not a girl I barely ever spoke to who shared her name with sweet and sticky candy.

"Are you okay?" she asked in her syrupy voice, hugging some books to her chest and batting her lashes pitifully. She wore a short black and white polka dot skirt and a loose-fitting yellow blouse. If you squinted, she looked like a bumble bee, buzzing around our table, feigning sympathy for the poor kid who lost her sister. She was, in short, a phony!

"She's fine," Christy answered on my behalf.

"Hey Christy," Caramel waved, then stopped, locking eyes with Christie's shiny green orbs. "It's not Halloween yet, or did ya'll wake up from a coma and not know what day it was?"

Beside me, I could feel Christy's angry flames radiating. I was half expecting Sarah to defend her, but she circled a wisp of her hair in one hand nonchalantly and pretended to be eating her food. I knew it was her way of getting back at Christy for the comment she made earlier. Sarah always had sharp comebacks handy to fire off in seconds. This time, she remained mute and left Christy to defend herself... by herself. I sat in tense, stunned silence, unable to speak.

"No, it's not, but I could ask you the same question. Why on earth are you dressed in a costume?" Christy shot back standing up for herself. "Maybe you should... buzz off." Christy chuckled at her own joke while heads swung in her direction at the comment. Even Caramel looked taken aback, but quickly masked it with a fake smile before trudging off. I gave Christy an encouraging smile, and she let out a breath. It was Sarah who usually did the comebacks, and for the first time since I knew her, Christy had handled her own battle.

"Hey Jacqueline," another voice greeted me. My eyes shot up again and there, in all his glory, stood my five-year long crush, Robert. He was smiling at me, not wearing a pitiful look like everyone else, like I was some wounded wet dog kicked to the side of the curb. He looked at me like I was normal, like the Jacqueline who came to school every day, the one who gave out easy smiles, wore rainbow-colored dresses and chatted comfortably with her friends.

"Hey," was all I could manage to say.

"You look different; nice!" He commented. "I like it."

I managed a smile. It was hard to know if he was being honest or just polite. Not everyone would agree that my blonde hair, now turned an ugly shade of crow's black, and my eyes lined with something that looked like smudged coal, making my face look like a panda's, was exactly the kind of look one would describe as ***nice.*** He waved awkwardly, then walked off, trails of excited squeals from Sarah following after him. She started talking about the impressive inches he had added to his height. I would have blushed from the few seconds of interaction, but I just pretended to be happy, not to ruin Sarah's delight that tried to cast away the shadows of the awful mood I was in.

Chapter 3

After school, Christy and I rode home with her father, as usual; who, like everyone else, tried so hard to be nice to me. People were treating me like a was a fragile china plate sitting at the edge of the table ready to slip off and break at the slightest mistake they could make by saying what they weren't supposed to. They didn't know that I had already fallen to the floor and shattered the day death snuck into our house and took away my favorite person in the world, leaving me a broken mess with pieces too scattered to be glued back together.

Something lodged painfully in my throat, and I began to cough. Christy immediately handed me a bottle of water and I downed it, but it still burned, and the water did nothing to quench the fire.

"Are you okay?" Christy's Dad asked.

I could have sworn I was on the brink of tearing my hair out, yet all I did was nod. If anyone should ask me that question again, I would go nuts and scream. I was okay, I was fine, and the more they kept asking, the more I was slowly losing it.

"Are you eating well, dear? Would you like me to stop by a restaurant? We can have ice cream if you want," he offered.

Tired, I just rested my head against the window, not bothering to answer him. Christy urged him to just drive me home, for which I was grateful. It was really sweet that he cared, but food never seemed to sit well in my stomach anymore. A little was enough for me now. Mother was so swallowed up in her grief and too angry at me to notice that my clothes were getting too large for me, too loose around the waist.

But I was fine. That was all that mattered.

They dropped me off and I said my goodbyes, exiting the car as quickly as possible. Christy's house was about five blocks away, unlike Sarah who lived twenty minutes away from school in a fancy condo with her mother who was divorced. I took the spare key from under the flower pot and unlocked the door, the deafening silence of the house greeting me as I entered.

To be honest, the house had felt haunted since my sister died. I could still hear her heels clicking against the stairs as she hurried out the door. I could still hear the ring of her laughter and her whining to Dad. Her voice, her laugh, her whine, her shout overwhelmed me, and my heart rate picked up at an alarming speed. I plugged in my earpiece and blocked out the noise. There was a note on the fridge: "*I'm out*," it said. It was in mother's handwriting, scribbled and in a hurry. No, 'I love you.' No tiny heart at the end of the statement. Dad would be at work burying himself under a pile of accounts and sheets. The fridge was empty, and I pretended not to notice that recently my mother preferred to get her calories from liquor. I pretended not to notice the bottles stacked in the not-so-secret parts of the house, pretended not to notice how her breath reeked when she talked, and I especially pretended not to hear the arguments between my parents late at night about how she was beginning to have a drinking problem.

Funny how she was the one drinking and Dad was not; in many ways he was closer to both of us than she was, ironic as that was. Funny how we all dealt with the pain in different ways, all part of the gift death had brought forth with its presence.

Grabbing an apple and a bottle of water, I texted Dad to grab some Chinese on his way back from work. I knew he would be hungry, though I doubted I would be able to eat very much, even though Chinese food was my favorite. I climbed the stairs and headed to my room, stopping in my tracks when a gust of wind blew Sandra's door open. I stared at the immaculate room, exactly as she had left it and was afraid to take a step in. That same pain lodged at my throat again, and without thinking, my legs began moving into her room of their own accord.

She had chosen the soft colors of pastel blue and white, with furniture to match. Sandra was different. Most other girls in their teen years would have chosen pink. My room was pink, in fact; but Sandra had loved blue all her life. She said there was a special kind of peace that came with the color. The bed was still made, her books neatly stacked on her shelf, and pens lined up perfectly on her reading table. I was afraid to touch anything, but I was tempted to go through her drawers. I opened the top drawer of her desk, and there was a family album. On the first page, there was a photograph of the two of us; Sandra was eight and I was four. Both of us were blondes and we both had blue eyes; traits passed down to us from our mom's genes. We were smiling. I went through more photos; Sandra's elementary school graduation, her birthdays, her awards in Math competitions. As we grew older, our bond was as tight as ever. It was all there, like a movie of our life in pictures. She wanted to become a doctor and I had always dreamed about becoming an actress, just like my idol, Angelina Jolie. Sandra had been my biggest supporter. Even though I had been too nervous and shy to join the Drama Club, she had pushed me to go for it.

I slammed shut the album, my breath coming out in raspy gasps. I had a hunch I was becoming asthmatic, because lately, my lungs found it hard to inhale oxygen. I scrambled to my feet, and as I whipped my bag over onto my back, the backpack swept everything off her bedside table.

"Oh no," I gasped.

I tried to arrange the items just as I had found them, but my fingers were shaky, and my breathing was labored. I picked up a shiny blue book with a rose on the cover from the floor, then paused, skimmed through its pages and a memory rang in my head. Sugar, Sandra's best friend and Caramel's elder sister, had gifted Sandra a diary on her birthday and I had fallen in love with the starry, glittery hardcover so much that I begged Sandra to allow me to have it, but she would not. She was in love with it herself, despite its color. Now I held it in my hands, and I was surprised to see that the pages were still empty.

"I wonder why she never used it." I muttered aloud as I flipped through it from beginning to end.

"Jacqueline, are you home?" my mother's voice rang out from the stairs. Quickly, I unzipped my bag and shoved the diary into it just before she entered the room.

"Jacqueline…?" Her voice trailed off and the smile slid from her face when she saw Sandra's things on the floor. Her mouth went agape, and her face went white, *just like Sandra's when she died*, I thought.

"You're ruining it!" she yelled, and I almost jumped out of my skin.

"I'm sorry…"

"Sorry? If Sandra sees…," She stopped and exhaled. "She hates her room being messed up and you know it. I made sure nothing was touched and here you are messing with it!"

"Honey!" I heard my father's voice. I wondered what he was doing home so early. Maybe they had come home together. My father entered the room dressed in a light tan shirt that was loose-fitting enough to house the bulge of his belly and hang over his brown khaki pants below.

"What's wrong?" he asked.

"It's…," my mother began to cry. She dropped onto Sandra's bed, face down, and sobbed into the palms of her hands. "I'm sorry. I didn't mean to yell."

My Dad went immediately to her side, sat down next to her and pulled her up, wrapping his arms around her. She nestled up against him letting her head rest on his broad shoulder as he rubbed a soothing hand up and down her back. He beckoned to me with his other hand to sit on his other side, but I shook my head and walked out of the room. I'd had enough pity for one day. I locked myself in my room, refusing to come out even when I heard knocks, and despite my empty stomach crying out for food. I slept off and on until late evening.

Chapter 4

The nightmare woke me, and I shot up from the bed, panting and sweating. It was always similar, dreams of Sandra the night she died, of her laying still and suddenly grabbing my arm and screaming, "Help me!"

In the darkness, the moonlight poured through the open window and cast what looked like moving shadows in my imagination. My body went cold with fear, as one of the shadows seemed to be approaching me, floating. Quickly, I switched on my bedside lamp, but there was nothing in the room. No shadows. Nothing. It was all part of my overactive imagination, playing with me in the darkness.

As the nightmares were continuing to be more and more frequent, my haven was slowly turning into a hell and sleep was now something I was scared of. I exited my room immediately and ran down the stairs. My frightened state must have scared my parents, and both of them dropped their separate chores and looked my way.

"I can't…" I whimpered.

"Jacqueline, honey," My mother called, taking off her apron and rushing to my side. I tried to pry her hands off me, but her grip was firm as she pulled me close.

"Leave me be!" I screamed. My heart was picking up its pace again, and I could feel its painful thump against my ribcage.

"Listen, honey, you've got to talk to me, or your father, or someone else. You can't go on like this." My mother was crying again, and she would not let go of me.

"Elizabeth, let me talk to her," my father intervened.

My head was reeling, their voices were fading and in my chest was a painful pounding.

"I don't want to talk," I said, but my voice sounded weak, defeated like it didn't belong to me.

"Jacqueline, Honey," my father said, pulling me gently from my mother's arms into his. He was the one holding me now. "We're going to the doctor's. You're not well."

"No!" I just needed them to keep quiet. Why did they not understand that I wanted to be left alone?

"Jacqueline..."

That was all it took for me to rush out of the house and into the street. I could hear their voices calling after me, but I kept running. The monster of my reality was trapped inside me, and no matter how far or fast I ran, it kept pace with me. I wanted to run from the nightmares, run from the yells and morning fights with my mother, run from the void my sister had left in the house and in myself. I ran and ran, but the more I did, the more it caught up with me. I could even hear Sandra's voice right behind me; and if my eyes weren't so blurry with tears, or I had not been screaming to block out her voice, or maybe if it had not been so dark, I would have seen the raised brick I had always avoided in front of Miss Jessica's house. I would have not caught my foot on it.

I fell on my elbows, but my knees were not spared from the impact. My whole body was sore, and I could not get up. I laid there on the curb, lonely and wounded, just as everyone saw me. That was all it took for me to burst into tears. I wish I understood it, those tears, why they kept pouring and pouring now, why I couldn't bring myself to get up and keep running. I cried a river from my heart, and oceans of salty tears from my soul. I didn't even hear the engine of a car approaching, or the footsteps of some teenage girls who were obviously coming from a party at that late hour of the night.

"Oh my God! Is she okay?" one of them spoke.

"Shush," another one answered. "She's hurt."

One of the girls crouched by me, and soon, thin arms were wrapped around me. There was a mixture of strong perfume tinted with the smell of booze from her, but her arms were all the comfort I needed. Soon, my cries turned to sobs, and I rested against her, imagining, just for a moment, that it was my sister's arms around me, like she used to do when I was too scared to sleep at night or woke up from a nightmare.

"It's okay," the girl whispered, and my sobs continued.

Just for a moment, I stayed like that, just until the police sirens blared in the air and I heard the sound of my parent's panicky voices as they rushed to me.

Chapter 5

Mrs. Gilbert, the therapist, was just how I pictured she would be; motherly, bespectacled, and eerily calm. She reminded me of my third-grade teacher, a woman I never liked because of all the stories she told us about her eight cats and how she was curing one of the little darling's bowel problems. The office was suffocating. It consisted of two swivel chairs and a desk, the contents of which were meticulously arranged, a couch, and two other single colorful chairs.

We each took our positions in one of the bright chairs and faced one another. There were posters on the wall about mental health and its importance, and some motivational statements that screamed words like, "You can do it!"

"Believe in yourself." "Change your thoughts to change your world."

"So, Jacqueline, on a scale of 1-10, how do you feel today?" she asked.

She had explained some stuff to me earlier, about how she liked asking her patients about rating their feelings on a scale, 1 being extreme sadness and 10 bursting with joy. I continued to look at her blankly as I had since the first moment I walked into her office.

Never in my twelve years of existence would I have imagined myself going to the therapist. After my parents found me that night, the very next morning they immediately booked an appointment with the therapist our neighbor had recommended. This was after I was taken to the hospital to be bandaged for my sidewalk spill. I didn't protest like I was supposed to, I guess I was just too tired to do so.

My mother walked on eggshells around me now. She called my school to tell them that I would not be attending for the rest of the week, and still I did not protest. She cooked my favorite meals and stocked them up in the fridge, and when she came to my room and I pretended I was asleep, she'd kiss me goodnight and tell me she loved me. I knew she did so because she was afraid that I might hurt myself again.

My mother did not love me, at least not the way she loved my sister. Sandra was always her favorite. I could still remember how her eyes gleamed brighter and how her smile got wider when Sandra walked into the house after me. I remember how hugs were for Sandra first. I always took the second one that had the remnants of her love. Even now that Sandra was gone, I got none of that and sometimes my mother would still look on longingly over my shoulder when I stepped in from school as if Sandra would magically appear.

My father, on the other hand, had always been the softer one. I wasn't totally sure where I stood with him; was I loved dearly or did he just care for me a lot? He was easier to talk to and reason with though. The only difference now was that he barely smiled, and some days I'd catch him in the garden, staring at the red hibiscuses, Sandra's favorite flowers. I wondered if I had been the one to die instead, would Mother drink every day to drown her sadness and lash out at Sandra the way she did at me every morning? Would Father spend less time at work and more time at home to console Sandra on her loss? Would I be missed at all?

"Jacqueline?" Mrs. Gilbert, the therapist, called me. I swam back to the shore of the present from my sea of thoughts, remembering I was still inside this room where everyone believed this woman would help solve my problems.

"Did you hear what I said the first time?" she asked, and I nodded.

"Would you like to give me an answer?" I shook my head to that.

"Tell me about Sandra." She propped up her notepad on one crossed leg and held the pen on her right hand.

"There's nothing to tell," I answered. "She's gone."

"Were you two close?" She asked, and I nodded.

"Tell me about what Sandra loves doing," she said.

"There's nothing to tell," I repeated like a robot. "She's gone. She doesn't *love* doing anything anymore."

She scribbled something on her pad, and by my guess, it was something like, *really difficult to interact with and therapy would not make her open up no matter how much I tried.* The quicker the time passed, the better it would be for both of us. Mrs. Gilbert set down her glasses and gave me a smile.

"I'm only trying to help you, Jacqueline," she said softly. "And I can only do that if you talk to me, okay? Feel free to talk about anything. Let's not talk about Sandra or how you feel or all that stuff. Let's just talk about anything."

"Do you have problems, too?" That was the first question that popped in my mind.

Mrs. Gilbert looked pleased. "Yes, certainly I do."

"If you're a therapist and want to help me with my problems, then why do you also have problems?"

Mrs. Gilbert sat back and chewed a little on the end of her pen. "We all have problems Jacqueline. It's inevitable. What we can control is how we respond to them, and my job is to help you with that."

Her response made sense but imagine a world without problems. Would life be easier, or would people crave some bit of a whirlpool to tackle? Come to think of it, life was kind of like a video game. Problems come, tackle them, move unto the next level and tackle another.

"What if a person is the problem? How do you deal with that?" I asked.

"No one else is ever the problem, Jacqueline," she answered. "Not everyone will like you, but you focus on the ones that do."

"What if that means your parents as well?"

"Some parents find it difficult in expressing their love to their children, but it's hidden in their actions," she smiled again. "Something as simple as, 'Good night,' or 'Have you eaten? Have you gotten home safely?' All of that is enough to show they care and love you very much. It just may not seem like it."

I had gotten all of those when Sandra was alive. It was like she got the bread and I was okay to have the breadcrumbs. I loved her too, and I didn't mind getting the leftover love of my mom and even my dad. But now that there was no bread to hand out, there weren't even breadcrumbs left for me.

"Do you feel unloved?" the therapist asked.

I shrugged in response.

"Let's talk about school." I suggested instead.

"Okay, let's. Tell me about your studies and friends." the therapist went on.

"My best friends are Christy and Sarah." I sighed, looking over at the wall clock. 2: 31 pm. Twenty-nine agonizingly long minutes to go. It was better to just talk about school or I'd go crazy from all the questions she asked.

"Christy is a sweetheart, but she can be a bit awkward sometimes. She's what you can call a true friend, I guess."

The therapist nodded and jotted in her note pad, I guessed something that would be like, *Finally! I get some words out of her!* She stopped writing and looked at me, adjusting her glasses and waiting for me to go on.

"Sarah's really pretty, like Cinderella pretty. Some days I wonder why she's friends with us, she could easily go ahead and be friends with Caramel…"

"Caramel?"

"Yeah, Caramel, Sandra's best friend, Sugar's younger sister. I think their mother must have had a serious sweet tooth issue when she was pregnant."

Mrs. Gilbert chuckled softly at my comment and scribbled in her pad again, the faint smile lingering on her lips.

"So, don't you perceive yourself as pretty?" she asked.

"I am talking about my friends, not me," was my response. It was the annoying way she kept twisting everything back around to me.

"I know, Jacqueline." She was so calm. I threw my hands in the air in frustration, crossed my arms, uncrossed them again, then sat up straight. Why did I feel so bothered by such a question? Maybe I felt I was exposing too much, like why would a total stranger want to know my secrets and my insecurities? Particularly ones I have never voiced before.

Deep inside me, I knew what my answer would be. I have never felt like the pretty one. Sandra's birth must have taken all of mom's best genes and left only a little for me. Even though we were both blondes, my hair looked like it was colored with yellow poster paint, while Sandra's looked like the pictures of Goldilocks. Most days, my hair was a frizzy mess, and Sandra's was the kind you'd see on Instagram with the hashtag, #woke up like this. She was beautiful in every sense of the word. The pre-teen world was not so welcoming for me, pimples greeted my forehead, nose, and chin, but Sandra was blessed with was flawless skin.

As much as I didn't feel like the pretty one, I was honestly never jealous of Sandra. She was my sister and I missed those nights we'd apply anti-acne face masks. She would apply one only for my sake, her face was acne resistant. I missed those days she'd take me shopping and help me pick out my clothes. I missed her a lot. A whole lot. Every minute, in fact.

I toyed with my crow-black hair and wondered what Sandra would say if she could see it. She'd be shocked, no doubt, and maybe drag me to a salon for an actual dye job.

"Which of your friends are you closer to?" the therapist went on as the silence from her last question stretched, but I was out of words.

"If talking is too much for you right now, you might try writing your feelings down. Have you ever kept a diary?" she asked.

I shrugged, "I'm not much of a writer."

"Well, think about it. It can help you sort through your feelings," she replied.

Chapter 6

Three o'clock finally came and I was free from the confines of the office. I stopped short when I saw my mother waiting at the reception and she waved at me.

"I thought Dad was going to pick me up," I said once she approached me. I could have mistaken the look that passed in her eyes as hurt, but she just smiled at me again.

"He was, but I wanted to come instead," she said. "Should we go get ice cream? Or some frozen yogurt? French fries?"

I shook my head. "I'm vegan."

My mother looked confused. "No, you're not. You are? Since when?"

"Since a few minutes ago." I shrugged and walked out of the building with my mother following in what I imagine was confused silence. As we approached the car, she opened her car door and I jumped quickly into the passenger seat. At first, we rode in total silence, then I switched on the radio, rummaging through the channels, finally settling for an unknown rock and roll song.

"That's horrible," my mother said. "Please change that awful noise."

"I like it."

I watched her fingers scratch the steering wheel as if she ached so bad to turn it off, but she did not.

"So, how was therapy?" she asked, sounding all peachy.

"Okay."

"Did it help?"

When I looked at her, she seemed hopeful.

"Oh, it did," I answered. "I'm so ecstatic that I'm flying over the moon and drinking from a rainbow. I'll show you my pet unicorn later."

She sighed deeply. "Jacqueline…"

"What? Isn't that what you want to hear? The magic of therapy?"

"Your father and I are doing this to help you."

"I don't need help. I'm not crazy. And I'm not going to sit through another hour while I'm being asked personal questions the answers to which are none of her f**king business!"

"Language!" my mother warned.

"Oh, I'm sorry!" I repeated the swear word a couple of more times. "Where's the oopsie jar? I'll put in my pennies."

My mother ran a hand through her hair and kept driving with a death grip on the steering wheel. Her knuckles were turning white and her jaw was clenched.

"All the more reason why you need therapy," she said at last.

"I am not going again!" I stated emphatically.

"You don't have a choice, young lady. If Sandra were here, she would have wanted you to go as well."

I felt as though my heart squeezed tight in my chest. That was a very low statement for her to make. I could feel the angry tears pricking the back of my eyes as I glared at her.

"Don't guilt me like that," I told her. "Don't try to emotionally blackmail me by using Sandra. It's dishonorable."

My mother scoffed. "I would never do that. You're misunderstanding it. Sandra would have wanted for you to be okay after she'd gone."

"The same way she would have wanted you to stop drinking yourself to sleep and ignoring the fact that you have a daughter who is supposed to see you as her role model?" I shot back at her.

My mother said nothing after that, nor did she spare me so much as a glance all through the journey back home. The minute she parked, I flew out of the car and unlocked the front door to the house, running all the way up to my bedroom. I slammed the door shut, locked it, hopped into bed, and screamed into my pillow.

So much for therapy.

My phone began to ring, and without looking at the caller, I switched it off. Silence was all the company I needed at that moment. I sat up in my bed, and the first thing that caught my eye was the glittery diary belonging to Sandra. It peeked out from under my pile of books. For the life of me, I don't know why I decided to follow the therapist's advice; penning out my feelings as a way to heal. I took the diary and opened it, writing down all that came to my head.

I wrote about how angry I was; at Sandra for leaving so soon, at Mom for always picking fights with me, and at Dad for barely being there. I wrote about my therapy session that day. I couldn't write down the feelings I had the night I ran away from the house. It was a clash of too many ugly emotions and too much of a burden for the pages to hold.

I tried to write about how I felt at the moment, searching inside of me for anything. The first page was filled, and my hand hovered above it, thinking about how to express myself on the next page. It was useless because the very next page held my answers.

Blank and empty.

***

School gave me many distractions; at least studies did. The only sports I engaged in was PE, and that was because it was compulsory. People were still being uncomfortably nice, but I tried as much as I could to ignore them. It would wear off, eventually.

The only teacher I loved and will always love is Mr. Stanley. He taught mathematics, and when he heard about Sandra's death, he consoled me and then went back to being himself, not like the other teachers who would watch me walk out in the middle of class, just slip off without any punishment. It had its perks, especially in extremely boring classes, but it irked me nonetheless; it still spelled pity.

After math class, he stopped me from leaving to tell me he was giving me detention for not turning in my homework. Truth is, it was plain laziness and forgetfulness that made me not do it. Math was as simple as the alphabet to me.

"What if you give me thirty minutes and I finish all fifteen problems?"

"No!" Mr. Stanley said. "But how about we solve some problems for fun during detention?"

"Sounds cool!"

Only I would say something like solving math was fun, but it was. Sandra was never really good with numbers and had even asked me to help her with some of her homework. In exchange, she'd do my makeup for me. I especially loved her nail varnish designs. After making my nails a work of art, we'd take loads of selfies. Those were such good days.

I laughed, and Mr. Stanley looked at me with a raised brow. Mixed emotions swirled within me; my happy memories of Sandra combined with the overwhelming fact that no more would be created. Mr. Stanley must have guessed what was going on with me, but he gave me a stern look and I scampered out of his class.

Sarah and Christy were waiting for me, already changed into their PE clothes. Christy tugged at her shorts, which now were a bit too short for her long legs. Sarah on the other hand flaunted her beautiful legs in hers.

"What took you so long?" Sarah asked, stretching her body.

"Mr. Stanley had me sign for detention today," I said.

"I'll wait for you after school," Christy said in a heartbeat.

I smiled at her. "Thanks, Chris, but you don't really have to."

"I want to, Jacqueline."

Christy had always been the sweetheart that made me wonder what I did to deserve her in the first place. Sure, we practically grew up together, but I felt she had done so much for me than I had for her. She felt too… unreal to be real.

"I've got to get home early. I can't wait for you. I'm sorry," Sarah pouted.

"You don't have to wait in the first place," I told her. I didn't know what to make of her expression and didn't think about it. Seconds later, I was in my PE clothes, the shorts just about the same size as they were since I was eleven since I was not as blessed as my friends in the height department. Today we'd be playing soccer, the only sport where I could handle a ball without hitting someone in the face.

PE was the only closest thing I got to exercise or extra-curricular activities; my limbs were as stiff as mom's frozen Thanksgiving turkey. Coach Ashton had once asked me to join the soccer team after seeing me kick two goals in a row into the opposing team's net, but I declined. I did not have that much spirit or dedication, and most times after school I preferred going home. But perhaps soccer might not be so bad after all, seeing as the house I once called home was nothing to look forward to anymore.

Before my thoughts overwhelmed me, we joined the rest of our class in racing around the field for warm-ups. Soon, the game began, and today I decided to participate fully and not disinterestedly as I had been. I scored the first goal and got cheered. We paused for a break, and I went to get a bottle of water. That was when I saw a glimpse of her sitting on the bleachers.

Sandra.

Chapter 7

My neck whipped back in that direction so fast, but there was no one there. I could have sworn I saw her for a second. Maybe it was the trick of the light, but was I beginning to hallucinate?

"Jacqueline!"

Christy shook me and I jumped, startled. She wore a worried look and held my hand which had now turned cold.

"You look like you've seen a ghost," she said. Was it possible to really see ghosts?

"Jacqueline, talk to me." She squeezed my hands. "God! You're frozen! Should I tell Coach you can't participate in the second half?"

I shook my head. "No, um, I'll be fine."

Christy, being Christy, did not believe me, so she went to get water for me and stayed by my side until we played again. My eyes kept darting to the bleachers, and I played half-heartedly. My mind was mush. I tried to put my head back in the game, at least until I heard my name.

"Jacky."

It was a whisper close to my ear; my sister's voice. I panicked and kicked the ball to the opposing team. I looked around wildly. We lost a goal, and blames were thrown my way. I did my very best to break the tie and score for my team, but I heard it again.

"Jacky."

I looked around. Left and right. Up and down.

"Jacky."

No one called me 'Jacky' except Sandra, and I was close to losing my mind.

"Jacky! Jacky! Hey Jacky!"

The voice was louder now, and I was sweating profusely. I could feel my sight getting blurry from confusion and my head reeling in a spinning momentum.

"Jacky! Over here! Pass the ball!"

Anger boiled up in me when I saw the source of the voice calling me. Caramel was waving her hands at me, trying to push an opponent away, keeping me from scoring the goal. I left the ball, marched towards her and I threw a hard punch at her face. She screamed and fell, but I was not done yet. I grabbed her hair and hit her head on the ground, my rage blinding me.

"Don't call me Jacky! Don't ever call me Jacky!" I screamed over and over again. Someone lifted me away from her before I caused any more harm, but I kicked and scratched and screamed, I wanted to deal with her for causing me so much confusion.

"Don't call me Jacky, ever! Don't call me Jacky! Let me go! Let me go!"

My voice was getting hoarser and was thinning away as I was carried off the field. In my fit of rage, I saw a glimpse of Christy looking terrified and behind her, a lock of golden hair.

A lock of golden hair; just like Sandra's.

When Coach requested that my parents be called, both of them arrived in less than thirty minutes. He explained to them what had happened, my moment of hysteria, and I sat there quietly without uttering a word. My mother was weeping softly, ever the dramatic one, as my father rubbed a comforting hand on her back.

"Jacky is Sandra's nickname for her," my mother explained. So, once again, instead of being punished, I was let go, and my mother let it slip that I was going for therapy. As if the pity I got was not enough. Even detention was canceled for me since I was to go home and 'rest properly.'

Outside the office, Christy was waiting for me, sitting there tugging endlessly at her shorts. I walked past her and to my parents' car, but she still followed me.

"Are you okay, Jacqueline?" She asked me, but I did not offer her any response. My parents soon joined us, and when Christy was about to get in the car with me, I stopped her.

"I want to be alone," I told her.

"Okay," she said, giving me a hug. "Just call me if you need me or if you need anything."

Instead of my feeling thankful, I felt a trickle of irritation at her. She was just too good, and it was nauseating. She just saw me mug someone like a gangster and go haywire after. Is it possible for someone to exist without a mean streak in their body?

I got in the car and my father drove. The ride would have been a silent one, but my parents began to talk about adding extra hours to my therapy each week, like the one hour I got was not torture enough. They spoke like I wasn't there, like the subject's opinion didn't matter or as if I wasn't able to decide for myself. The sudden urge to run far away from them both overcame me, and I was tempted to open the door at the stop sign and follow that urge.

"Jacqueline, sweety," I cringed at the term of endearment my mother rendered me. "Would you like to eat anything? Your father and I are thinking Chinese, perhaps. You love Chinese."

"No. Both of you should not be hungry. You've had your fill from eating away my sanity," I said. My mother sighed, and my father took the next turn to the Chinese restaurant to order take out. As usual, when we arrived home, the first place I went was my bedroom. I completely ignored my mother's calls. I did my usual therapy of screaming into my pillow before I could calm down properly and followed it with my new therapy of writing.

As I opened the first page of the sparkly diary, nothing I had previously written was there. Instead, the words I saw nearly caused my soul to escape from my body.

Jacky help me.

Chapter 8

Dennis Chestnut.

The name didn't ring a single bell in my head, and many days I wished I had known him better.

When I was six, Sandra and I would look through photographs of our family, and I'd see some pictures of a man holding me as a baby. Sandra told me his name, Dennis Chestnut, and that he was our real father, and had been visited by death when I was a few months old. I had no memories of the dark-haired man that stared back at me, for the only man I had always called Daddy was Ben Lautner, my present Dad, who was actually my step-dad.

Sandra told me that sometimes she'd send him letters. She'd thought if she read it out loud to God that God would tell Dennis about his daughter missing him on earth.

That was the only close connection we had with the ones who were long gone. They never came back to Earth, and certainly did not come by my room and write in my new diary.

It takes a series of occurrences to trick your head into believing in coincidences, but the moment you start believing these things were more than coincidences, you were in for a much greater misery.

When I first took that diary, the pages were blank and untouched. I thought I had missed seeing the date at first that suddenly appeared in Sandra's handwriting, but the message had come in on a page I had filled with ink and I felt it was no coincidence. I didn't utter a single word about it to my parents while they kept on talking about my therapy, even over dinner. And I did not butt in, the noodles already cold from my stirring. I looked at my father; could he be the one playing a joke on me? Surely, it's not April Fool's, and it was impossible to play such an expensive and sick joke to cheer me up, especially at the expense of a dead girl. My mother would definitely not do something like that. Sandra's memory was too sacred for her to joke about.

"Mom, did Sugar come over today?" I asked my mother. She looked surprised by the question and patted her lips with a paper napkin.

"No, she didn't."

"What about any other day? Does she ever enter my room?"

"Jacqueline," my father replied sharply. "No one sets foot into your room. And besides, when Sugar comes over, she doesn't ever go upstairs anymore."

It was true. Sugar no longer roamed the house like she did when Sandra was alive. She would barely even stay for ten minutes before leaving. It was unbearable for her to stay here.

"Is something wrong? Something missing?" my dad prodded.

I shook my head and stuffed more cold noodles in my mouth, the spicy flavor that played on my taste buds was now gone with the heat. I had no appetite, but since I didn't want to add more things to 'worry' about to my parent's list, I decided to eat it all up. My mother smiled at me pleasantly, then continued eating her food.

That night we all stayed up late to watch reruns of the TV detective show, *Bones,* at my mother's insistence. I could have sworn we'd watched that show more than ten times and that I had practically memorized the lines of most of the episodes. It was all we ever watched on TV. I was seated between both of them, the 'perfect' family night.

I would have chosen the haven of my bedroom over this, but I was too scared to set foot into that room. On the TV, Bones and Angela were discussing the murder of a middle-aged man. Meanwhile, I was busy trying to track the sense behind the diary.

Does my sister's ghost still live on?

I almost laughed at the incredulity of my thoughts. Ghost? Really? We were on earth, not some fantasy world conjured up by a lame fiction writer. Ghosts do not exist, and the only reasonable explanation was that perhaps one of my parents had torn off the page and kept it, secretly planning to give it to the therapist in the hope that she could understand me better. The foremost suspect was my mother. She felt she had the right to breach my privacy any time she pleased.

But how did that explain the writing?

"I'm going upstairs," I said, standing.

"Okay," mom said. "But we're all going over to Caramel's tomorrow to apologize, okay?"

"And why should I?" I folded my arms.

"Jacqueline, please," my father pleaded. "It's the right thing to do."

Knowing it would only lead to an endless argument and me eventually being forced to go there anyway, I said nothing more and went up the stairs. Instead of going to my room, I opened the door to my parents' room and shut it quietly behind me. If my mother could invade my privacy, I could invade hers.

I started searching the drawers first. Nothing. Her bag. Nothing. Her wardrobe. Nada. No sign of any folded or scrunched up paper. I searched in between their books and even inside their shoes; but frustrated, I could not find a single thing. When I heard the door handle open, I slid into the closet and hid behind mom's dresses.

It was my father who had stepped in, and a loud fart followed. I peeked through the clothes, watching as he stood in the middle of the room, just staring into space like he always did since the incident. In a minute, he got down on his knees and rested his elbows on the edge of the bed. *When did my father become religious?* I wondered. I could hear his words clearly, and since his eyes were shut, I figured that it would be the perfect time to escape undetected.

I went on all fours and slowly pushed the closet door open. The carpet cushioned my knees and palms, so I was as noiseless as a mouse. It was when I was close to my victory that a statement in his prayers halted my movement.

"And Lord, please forgive me for what I said to Sandra. I'm sorry."

He began weeping at this point, and I quickly exited the room before he could open his eyes. His admission still baffled me. What did he say to my sister? Was it so bad that it turned him into a God-fearing, religious man? I felt there was no point in overthinking it. He probably said some hurtful words to her in the past that made him regretful. The more I tried to brush it off, the more the matter perched gnawingly on my shoulder. Curiosity was a dangerous thing, and I was curious to know what my father had said that was so horrible.

The dreaded moment of having to enter my room came. I stood before my door which was wide ajar. I was thinking about asking my parents to allow me to sleep in their room instead, but that would only mean I was confirming my fears of non-existent beings. My steps were forced. The diary gave off a glittering light, still laying in the middle of my bed where I had left it since that afternoon. Perhaps I could go to Christy's for a last-minute sleepover. That would not be such a bad idea.

Jacqueline, you're scared.

Honest thoughts rang in my head. The truth I had tried to bury resurrected itself and it was chilling me to the bone. I shivered from an unknown cold. Grabbing the dairy, I opened my window, flung the little book out as far as I could and shut the crosshatched panes of glass so hard, they shook from the pressure.

Better.

The day's stress weighed on me and there was no, non-existent, creature that would stop me from getting my sleep that night.

Chapter 9

I was back in the prison of Mrs. Gilbert's office for another session of therapy. My parents had finally gotten their way, adding two extra hours and three days a week after school, starting the very next week after my Caramel incident. My ever-cheerful therapist was smiling at me, and I was counting the seconds left until I would be allowed to leave.

Fifty-five minutes and five seconds, four seconds, three...

"So, how was school this week?" she asked, after asking the usual questions about my overall well-being and what "number" my happiness sat at.

I shrugged. "Hit someone really badly. Had to apologize."

"And how does that make you feel?"

"Well, she looked prettier with the black ring around her eye."

"What provoked this hit?"

"She called me Jacky."

The therapist looked interested. "Jacky?"

"Yeah. Only Sandra calls me that," I said.

I guess the fact that I would have to keep coming here until the end of eternity or until I got better was what motivated me to keep talking. It's only when there was progress that I'd be freed from this torture of a conversation every week.

"Caramel calling me that provoked me, and that was how best I could respond. I had no control over it," I sighed.

"Okay!" she scribbled into her notepad, and I was guessing it was something along the lines of *'troubled child who finds joy in hitting people.'*

"Caramel is Sugar's younger sister. Sandra's best friend, right?"

I nodded in affirmation.

"How's your relationship?"

I checked the time again. Fifty-three minutes and forty-three, forty-two, forty-one seconds...

Too damn slow.

"We aren't all that close," I scrunched my brows. "Scratch that, we aren't close at all."

"Was Caramel the first person you'd ever hit?"

I nodded. I have never been violent in any way, even verbally, much less getting to that level of physical. I was thinking about talking about the diary incident with the therapist, maybe they'd have some psychological term for all of that. However, if I did, I knew it would drag on and on and probably into the next session, which I was trying to avoid as much as possible. I wanted to cover the grounds of my fight in today's session, one and done, and move on to another aspect of my craziness in the next. Then my big plan was to fake happy expressions and joviality until I was rendered okay and depression free.

Well, I wasn't exactly diagnosed with depression yet, but a few more sessions and I figured we'd go there.

I have never hated Caramel, nor have I liked her. We were more on civil grounds. Well, Christy, Sarah, and I were, but she was inclined to reign with the evil intent of making life miserable for us even though it was ever so subtly.

"Do you get the urge to hit someone sometimes?" she asked.

"Can we stop talking about violence?" I said, already bored. "Ask me something else, like, 'Would you like to end this session now and I tell your parents you're a super okay kid with no case of loose screws in her head?"

Mrs. Gilbert smiled and put down her notepad. If she was actually going to say that, I'd thank her profusely and perhaps give her a cat recipe.

"Sometimes I forget you're twelve," Mrs. Gilbert said. "Pardon me for saying that, but you speak in a quite remarkably adult manner for your age."

I did not expect that. I had been nothing but a rude, stuck-up girl.

"Uh… thanks?"

Mrs. Gilbert smiled again, like she always did, then took up her notepad again and looked at me.

"Let's do word association."

"Word what?"

"Word association," she reiterated. "I'll say a word, and you say the first thing that comes to your mind at the mention of that word, okay?"

I nodded. "Okay." Great. A game. Better than 20 questions.

"Alright," she cleared her throat, then took a while to write in her notepad. She looked up at me again. "Now, we begin. Comfort…"

"Bedroom?"

"Exactly." She gave a small clap. "I want immediate answers, okay? Let's continue. Truth."

"Reality." I responded.

"Bitter."

"Reality."

"Love."

"Chinese food."

"Hate."

"Pity."

"Pretty."

"Sarah."

"Sweet."

"Christy."

"Happiness."

"Sandra."

"Sadness."

"Sandra," I whispered the last word, an unexpected catch in my voice. The therapist watched me for a while and jotted in her notepad.

"We'll continue this further. Tell me more about Sandra."

The session ended eventually, and mom was waiting to pick me up in reception again. She looked better now that she was rarely sporting the 'emotionally drunk mother' look. She and Mrs. Gilbert spoke awhile while I waited. I knew there was this secrecy oath or patient privacy stuff therapists were sworn to, so I had no reason to worry, I guess. After a few minutes, mom drove us home. A silent ride, for which I was immensely grateful.

"What do you say, this weekend, you, your Dad, and I take a break and go someplace nice?" She suggested after parking the car when we got home.

I paused as I was halfway out of the vehicle. "Where?" I asked, a mix of curious and suspicious.

"You get to pick." My mother smiled. Looking at her up close, she was indeed looking so much better. There were no alcohol bottles stacked in different corners of the house anymore. When I grew older, I planned to make sure to stay away from that stuff because the effects it had were horrible. Why didn't people say stay away from alcohol as much as they say you should stay away from drugs?

"Can we go visit Uncle George and Aunt Margaret?"

Uncle George was Dad's brother-my current Dad-who owned a campsite. He was, along with Mr. Stanley and my two best friends, one of my favorite people in the world. He always had jokes and tall tales up his sleeves, and he loved to cook out on his grill. Thick seasoned steaks and smoked chicken; his food was always the best. Aunt Margaret made the best apple pies too, which made my mouth water just thinking about it.

"Okay, we'll go Friday after school; how's that?" My mother asked and I nodded.

I got out of the car and trudged up the walk into the house. Ever since tossing the diary a couple of nights before, I felt relieved that I wouldn't have to deal with that irrational fear any longer. I could have simply asked my mother for the torn-out page, but she seemed to be trying so hard to make things work between us I saw no reason to start a fight. She even baked the night before, which was rare, and even though the cake was dry and not very flavorful, it was a very sweet effort on her part.

Chapter 10

Friday came quickly and the warmth of the summer sun embraced us softly as we packed for the trip. It was about a three-hour drive, give or take, to get up to my aunt and uncle's. I was allowed to invite my friends along on the trip which made things even more relaxed and pleasant, and Christy looked more excited than any of us. She was already snacking on the treats we packed for the long road trip and I was afraid she might end up with an upset stomach from all the junk food before we even got there.

"We'll have a campfire again, right?" Christy asked, clapping excitedly as my father drove.

"As long as I sleep under a mosquito repellent net or have a bug light, I think I'll be fine." Sarah said.

She did not share half as much of Christy's enthusiasm, and her enormous bag was the heaviest out of all of ours. It looked like she packed as if she was going on another vacation to France.

"We have plenty of ammunition for those pesky mosquitoes, sweetie," mother laughed.

She threw me a genuine smile and I returned it back. A mini vacation was what we all needed to escape the prison of our loss, and nothing was more calming than being surrounded by nature. Christy had often told me how it was strange for someone like me to find peace in nature. She always thought of me as more into loud music and urban scenes. But sometimes, the soul calls out to the beauty of Mother Earth, a beauty that surpasses all others. Maybe I had the soul of an old hippie at heart.

"We can go swim in the lake!" Christy clapped again.

"Ducks swim in that lake and they poop in them as well," said Sarah, the killjoy.

"And the barbecue!" Christy continued her confounded clapping and I felt a headache coming on. "Please tell me Uncle George will barbecue!"

"A fly could land on the meat and be grilled along with the barbecue! Remember that and check your food." Sarah said.

"The starry nights," Christy sighed.

"I still believe a bear lurks around that perimeter, "Sarah said. "I heard a growl one night the last time we were up there."

While one kept talking about the many joys of the place and the other, unsuccessfully, tried to kill those joys, my parents were getting a kick out of the banter and were laughing at them both. Eventually, all three of us girls wore ourselves out and we nodded off. We arrived at the campsite in three hours and thirty minutes and I was shaken awake. I felt something wet on my bare shoulder and woke to see that Christy had rested her head on my shoulder and drooled down my arm in her sleep.

"Christy!" I yelled and her eyes snapped wide awake.

"We're here!" she screamed, and my father covered his ears in an effort to prevent his eardrums from shattering. Sarah woke up and drew back the curtain of her hair, grumbling as she slowly stretched and stepped out of the vehicle. Uncle George was the first to come to greet us, his friendly, happy vibes instantly livening our tired spirits. He hugged my mother first, then my father, and lastly hugging me against his protruding belly. When I was younger, I used to think men got pregnant based on the size of Uncle George's tummy, but he told me he saved food in there for winter.

Later, I realized it was a thing in my Dad's family, men with big bellies that housed nothing but too much food.

"Uncle George!" Christy yelled and practically jumped on him. You'd think she was his niece and not me.

"My little squirrel," he laughed.

"Not so little anymore, am I?" She twirled.

"Surely not," he replied then looked over at an uncomfortable Sarah. "What's wrong, Darling?"

Sarah shook her head. "I'm fine."

"Come on in and we'll we serve you our best crocodile sauce," he invited us. "Margaret's been dying to serve you all. Caught one in the pond last night."

Sarah looked both horrified and disgusted, and Christy and I looked at each other for moral support as if to say, *no way!*

"Just kidding!" he guffawed, and my parents joined in. Christy's laugh was unusually high-pitched and exaggerated, while Sarah looked like she was going to cry.

"Kids go on inside, I'll take care of the luggage," Dad said.

"Thanks, Dad." I appreciated that he was working so hard to make things nice for us. Before Christy could run into the cabin, I grabbed her arm and stopped her.

"You did not sneak more candies than you were supposed to, right?" I asked. "Or did you hug Caramel for too long?"

"What?" She shook her head. "No, and **_definitely_** no! Why?"

"You've been crazily happy like you're on a sugar high," I told her.

"Well…" She dragged on and looked left and right; anywhere else but at me.

"Well?" I urged on.

"It's just… I really miss you, Jacqueline," she confessed.

I was confused. "How? I'm right here! And you see me almost every day in school."

"No, I just miss the Jacqueline before…"

Her words hung in the air, and I let go of her arm, realizing what she meant.

"And you figured by being excited with this trip I'll come back?" I asked her.

"I was hoping you would," she said with an earnest honesty. "You were exactly as happy as me when we'd come visit here."

She was right. Coming over to Uncle George's made me very happy, bringing out an ecstatic and crazy side of me I tucked away most of the time. Sandra would try to shut me up as I sang annoying songs on the way and would give up and beg my parents to ask me to stop.

"But you're happy we're here, right?" she asked.

I nodded. "I've haven't been this happy since…" I shrugged. "Well, you know."

Christy smiled, her green contacts shining brighter outdoors. Sarah walked up to us.

"Was your uncle joking about catching a crocodile or cooking crocodile sauce?" she asked.

"I don't know, but I bet the sauce would taste awesome!" Christy clapped.

"I'm not eating a single meal here. I stuffed enough carrots in my bag to last me for a day," Sarah said.

Aunt Margaret showered my face with kisses as I stepped into the kitchen. There was a large pot boiling angrily over the stove, the foamy hot liquid pushing up the lid threatening to erupt like a volcano. Food was served in no time, and even Sarah could not resist the array of delicacies my aunt spread out on her table. Crocodile meat or not, it tasted heavenly. We all ate to our hearts' content, and Sarah even succumbed to the calories of the sweet goodness of my aunt's desserts.

Dad and Uncle George talked outside after lunch, and my mother and Aunt Margaret busied themselves in the kitchen, giving us permission to go and have fun. Our first go-to place was the pond, a fairly large body of water that separated Uncle George's place from the huge cabin he used as a rental for other people. The ducks loitered around peacefully, and some birds swooped down to take a bath in the warm water. Their peace was disrupted when Christy and I cannonballed into the lake, fully-clothed, garnering annoyed quacks directed at our antics.

"I've missed this so much," Christy said, dipping into the water and resurfacing.

"Me too," I agreed.

Sarah screamed a little when a duck got too close to her and walked at a faster pace to come nearer to the edge of the lake.

"Come swim!" I invited her in, but she shook a finger at us.

"That water is not hygienic," she said.

"Oh Sarah, if we worry about what's hygienic and what is not, we'd never have any fun!" Christy swam towards her direction.

"And nothing can ever be a hundred percent hygienic," I added.

Sarah looked longingly like she wanted to join as she watched us splashing water on each other. She sat on the bank, toying with the grass until we directed our water splashing to her. Once again, just like at the table, she ignored all of her self-made rules and jumped into the water with us.

Chapter 11

I felt ten times better after two nights at Uncle George's. I slept well, ate well, and enjoyed nature, my friends, and my family. I felt several steps closer to normal and I was grateful for that.

Sunday morning, we were packed up and got ready to go, and if time machines existed, I'd have loved to go back and relive those happy moments again. It had been such a long time since laughter had rung from any of us, and I had forgotten how beautiful Mom looked when she laughed; how Sandra looked so much like her. Somehow it made me happy, seeing her like that, like the mother I knew before. It was almost like seeing Sandra laugh, and deep inside me, I knew that I would give anything to see that every day.

Aunt Margaret's meals were so delicious, which made Sarah forgot her dieting and calories and eat like she'd die tomorrow. It had been a long time since she had a home-cooked meal. Her mother was always too busy, and the kitchen was never even touched anymore. Christy was calm and her smile was wider than I had seen it in months. I felt it was not only a great weekend for me but for my friends as well.

We were standing in front of my Dad's car, waiting for Dad who was still inside talking with Uncle George. Sarah was checking her hair in the mirror, and Christy's eyes were trailing a yellow butterfly that passed by her, watching it kiss the sweet nectar of a sunflower. Aunt Margaret approached us holding a covered plate, and at once Sarah tucked away the mirror, she was using to fix her lipstick and looked hungrily at it.

"Is that the pineapple upside down cake?" she asked. She spoke so fast I wondered how her words didn't tumble over each other or how Aunt Margaret had heard and understood her.

"It sure is," she said. My mother stepped forward and took the cake, Sarah's eyes following its path. I was sure she was salivating and aching to pounce on it like a hungry lion.

"And a little extra piece for you, Sarah," Aunt Margaret winked as she handed her a piece of cake in a little foil wrapping. Sarah practically barked her thanks and took the huge slice from her. She unwrapped it and ate it immediately, closing her eyes as she savored the product of the magical hands of Aunt Margaret. We all stood watching her, and when she opened her eyes, her cheeks went red making us all burst out laughing.

Dad came to join us a little while later, apologizing profusely for keeping us waiting. Uncle George surprised me by putting his two strong hands on my waist and throwing me up in the air, earning a frightened scream from me.

"Someone is still scared of heights," he guffawed, clearly enjoying it at my expense.

"Put me down!" I yelled. He did so, still laughing, and my heart had taken a wild race. Heights were the things that frightened me the most, it was probably a fear I was born with, or possibly developed from Uncle George who thought every kid liked the idea of being thrown up as high as the heavens and caught like it was a sport to him. Sandra told me I had acrophobia, meaning heights scared the hell out of me.

"To get over your fears, you have to face them," he patted my shoulder.

I was about to say someone should grab me a pen and paper while I write that down so I could frame it to hang among the dozen other motivational quotes in my therapist's office, but I held my tongue when I realized Christy and Sarah were present. I didn't want them to know I went for therapy, because I was not crazy, and therapy was never my choice.

I instead, nodded at him. He probably thought his words had some mighty profound effect on me because he nodded too, as if there was a connection, then patted my shoulder twice.

"We'll see you coming around more often, won't we?" Aunt Margaret asked Dad.

"Sure."

My Dad smiled. His tummy even looked bigger over just the short time we'd spent there. I was going to have to put out the idea of Dad and me going for an early morning jog every day to help him lose that belly fat. Soon, there were departing regards and we were on the road back home. Car rides were soothing enough for Christy to lull her to sleep and she made a stream of drool down my arm again.

We dropped Sarah off first, and then we stopped over at Christy's, deciding to stop in and say hi to her family. I did protest, mostly because as nice as Christy was, her brother Eric was the complete opposite of her; irritating, annoying, and a complete bully. I never talked or asked about him and wished he was as far as the North pole instead of just a few blocks away. Even if I got the chance to save up enough money to hire kidnappers to dump him in that cold zone, I feared for Christy's happiness. She seemed to like him, so sadly, he'd have to stay. Or maybe Christy would support the idea. He did bully her, as well, after all.

"Wassup Voldemort?" He asked me, taking in my outfit.

That was still the nicest compliment I had ever gotten from him, but Christy said he was just being nice because he was afraid, I was still shaken and fragile from my sister's death.

"Hey, Lucifer!" I greeted back.

Eric smiled at that. He and Christy bore no resemblance to one another at all. No one could tell she was related to the popular Eric Edgewood. Physically, Eric was tall and broad, had a social life. His hair was as wavy as any of the models adorning the front of one of the stashes of *Vogue* magazines Sandra had, and he was great at sports. Luckily for him, he also had perfect 20/20 vision, while Christy was practically what you'd call legally blind. Her brown eyes, now artificially green from contacts, could not see well enough to kick a ball into the goal to save her life without her optical aids and the most fun she got was from studying and hanging out with Sarah and me.

Eric and Sandra were in the same class and had been friends too. I wondered if he missed her as much as I did. I did see him at the funeral looking so forlorn, and it was very foreign to see the absence of that smirk that was permanently plastered on his face. I once overheard Sugar and Sandra talking about him and my sister confessed to having a crush on him. There was a great urge to run into the toilet and puke my guts out after hearing that. Sure, he fell under the category of being *close* to handsome, but his annoying traits denigrated his looks and all I could see was…

Well, Lucifer as I called him.

"Miss me?" he went on.

"Your absence? Yeah," I replied. He put a hand on my head and ruffled my hair as I stood there exhaling with loud exasperation, hoping the torture of visiting would be short.

"Leave her alone, you doofus," Christy pushed his hand away.

Eric pouted and feigned a hurt expression. "But I missed her."

"Go find someone your own size," Christy told him off while dragging me by one hand up to her room. I looked over at Eric and there was a mischievous grin playing on his lips, leaving me to wonder in torture trying to figure out what tricks he had up his sleeves.

Christy's room was as messy as ever. That was what made her room hers, messiness, and yet still it was comfortable to be there. I had missed it, messiness and all, and leapt onto her bed strewn with as many clothes as were on the floor. Christy laid down next to me and we both stared up at her ceiling, saying nothing and enjoying the silence.

"I told my parents I want a new little brother or sister," she said, breaking the silence.

"Eww."

"Oh, come on, Jacqueline, there's nothing 'Eww' about it."

She sat up and her face hovered above mine.

"Okay, I think I might be desperate for one if I was related to Eric," I said, to which she giggled.

"And what did they say?"

"You know, they laughed it off awkwardly." She shrugged. "It would be great to have a baby sister, though. Don't you want one?"

"You mean those little things that cry when they poop and poop when they cry?"

Christy laughed. "You've watched too much Shrek, but yes."

I shook my head. "Nope."

The silence returned and Christy began toying with the sleeve of her sweater, pulling gently at a loose thread. It was obvious she had more to say. She finally looked at me with those eerily disturbing eyes and said, "Doesn't it get lonely sometimes, Jacqueline?"

The silence grew thicker now from my lack of response. I looked at Christy, and she was guiltily biting her lower lips, an unconscious self-retribution she does when she would rather take back her words but can't. I sighed, and there was no point in not being plain honest with her.

"It does," I admitted. "I'm lonely almost all the time. Some days it's because of the nightmares and the fact that I can't tell anyone about them. Some days it's the fact that when I wake up from these nightmares there is no one to hug me and tell me it's going to be okay. Some days it's the emptiness of the house. So yes, Christy, it gets lonely sometimes. Very lonely."

Christy went back to her former position next to me and laid her head on my shoulder. She was probably thinking I would cry after letting all that out, but I had long exhausted my emotional dam of tears and found there was no peace in crying. It only made a situation a whole lot worse.

"You know," Christy started. "You can always call me up when you have a nightmare. I know it's at night, probably even really late, but I'm a light sleeper."

I shook my head at the idea. "Thanks, Christy but…"

"I'll sing you a song 'til you fall asleep," Christy persisted. "It's what Eric does when I have a nightmare, but I don't have them frequently though."

It was not the sweet gesture of Christy singing to me in the middle of the night that got me to shoot straight up from my position, but the fact that her devil of her brother sang her songs.

"Which Eric? Your brother?" I wanted to be sure.

Christy laughed and sat up too. "Yes, Jacqueline, that same Eric that opened the door for us."

"Wow!" I should have said more but that was all I could say, just 'wow.' When did the devil possess an ounce of softness in his heart? Was he the typical kind of bad boy in books who fought physically and are complete douchebags but on getting to know them they had hearts as soft as pillows and all that bravado was a mask?

Nah, that only existed in fiction.

"He's annoying, but he's sweet." Christy giggled again. "He'd kill me if he ever heard me describe him this way. And please, don't mention anything about his singing, please."

"Of course not," I laughed when she begged me earnestly. "I bet he's a really horrible singer."

"Actually..." Christy continued on. "He's a pretty good one. Great, if I'm not exaggerating."

I just raised a brow at that and said nothing. Next thing she might say is that Eric wakes up in the morning before everyone and makes them a breakfast buffet when all I've seen him do is eat ramen uncooked because he was too lazy to boil water and drop them in.

"So..." Christy beamed.

"So...?"

"About a baby brother or sister?"

"Still no." I said immediately. "I love my sanity the way it is, thank you very much."

Christy scooted closer and set her voice in a whisper. "I have a feeling my Mom's pregnant, Jacqueline."

My eyes perked open wider. "Really? What makes you think so?"

"She was puking all morning," she said.

"Well, must be the sight of your brother," I said, and she hit my arm lightly at that. "I also have a feeling about something, Christy."

She scooted so close to my face her nose was almost touching mine.

"Yeah?" she was impatient to hear what I had to say.

"I think my Dad's pregnant too." We both burst out laughing after that.

Chapter 12

Eric came up to tell me that my parents were set to go home. I wanted to ask if I could stay over with Christy for just that night, but I was seriously craving some alone time and Satan lived in the bedroom next to Christy's. The moment I stepped out of her room, something soft and wet was pressed beneath my feet. I looked down, then let out a scream and I tried to kick the poop off my shoes. Eric was standing there and laughing his head off, and Christy did not know what to do, so she screamed along with me, which was not very helpful.

"Get it off me!" I told him.

"Watch where you're going next time, Maleficent," he grinned. "And by the way, it's just chocolate, and a few other things."

I stepped out of my shoes and skirted around the mess on the wooden floorboards. For a moment I stood there glaring at him. He was so enjoying this. Christy shoved him hard in the chest, but he didn't even budge.

It was hard to believe this was the sweet brother Christy had talked about.

"I really hate you, Eric Edgewood," I told him and took the tissue paper that Christy had gone to fetch me and attempted to clean the mess off the floor.

"Feeling's mutual, Vampire."

There was so much relief once I cleaned up my shoes and left the house. Christy promised to call me later in the day. The minute I entered the car, I asked the question just as it popped into my head.

"Mom, have you ever thought of having another child?"

Mom and Dad turned to look back at me simultaneously, then Dad turned back in silence and focused on the road until we arrived at our house.

"Another baby? Why ask that all of a sudden, sweetheart?" my mother asked.

She looked like I had hit her with the greatest surprise. She was not even that surprised on Christmas when Sandra and I got her the Turkish vintage scarf that she loved so much it was literally her trademark.

I shrugged, ignoring the way her eyes bore into me.

"Just asking."

My mother nodded, but she was clearly not buying it. Her confusion was later replaced with sadness, which was evident from her slouched shoulders and far off gaze. Maybe I was too insensitive. They had just lost a child and I was asking for another. There could be various worst-case scenarios; a miscarriage or a stillbirth when another seed of joy was blooming, and it could suddenly be uprooted. It would wreck my mother and Lord knows I did not want it to come to that.

I'd become so darkly cynical and such a pessimist. I needed work on my positive thinking skills if I didn't want to remain in therapy for a year or more.

"I don't want another brother or sister, Mom," I said. "All I did was ask."

"I know, I know," she said.

"Honey," my father called to me. "Why don't you take the cake on inside the house and have a slice?"

I got out and took the cake from Mom. Her eyes still had that far off look even when she looked right at me. It was like she was seeing through me, past me to some distant space. I walked over to the house throwing a glance back over my shoulder at my parents and I could see them conversing in the car. There was no room for guilt. All I did was ask her if she ever thought of it as casually as I could, and I had not expected such a reaction from them.

I set the cake down on the dining room table, took a knife and cut out a huge chunk. Mom was not much of a sweet tooth, so it was probably Dad and me who'd finish it. I hummed a melody from some song I'd heard that was stuck in my head as I stuffed the yummy pastry in my mouth and jogged up the stairs. It felt like we had been away from this depressing house for a week, and I felt much better. I bet my therapist would sense that and figure out I no longer needed therapy. How else could one convince those mind readers when they've mastered how humans work?

I unlocked my door and tossed my bag on the floor. I was just about to hop on the bed when something caught my attention.

Something glittery.

The diary was back, and in the exact same place it had been before I threw it out the window.

The cake dropped out of my hand.

Chapter 13

The Exorcist.

It was a book written by William Peter Blatty, one of the best horror books of all time. Recently, I was scrolling through Instagram and I came across a post about a man who had pranked his mother-in-law. His mother-in-law had bought this book and could not finish reading it because it was too full of evil. She ended up throwing it in the sea because she could not sleep under the same roof with such a book. Her son-in-law, the prankster, bought a new copy of the book, put it under running water to wet it and placed it by her bedside table when she was asleep. His father-in-law told him that that was the first time she had ever screamed and fainted in her life. I remember laughing at how funny it was, tears coming out from my eyes at the wicked yet hilarious prank the man played on the poor old lady, but I realized it was not the least bit funny when it was happening to me and it was in no way a prank.

When I saw the book there again, I started to believe that everything I had been seeing, hearing, and dreaming about were all connected, and this was no longer my imagination as I had seriously hoped it was. The house had been empty. There was no sign of breaking in or forced entry, so how else could I explain how the diary was back on my table?

To say that I was freaked out would be a gross understatement. A more accurate depiction was that my soul ran out of my body from fear and I froze in my tracks. I didn't hear my mother call me, and even after she stepped into the room and saw the diary and took it back to Sandra's room, I didn't say or do anything. I wanted to tell her to keep it out of the house, that it was a strange object, but my mother would have me locked up in a mental health facility in fear that I might be running mad if I told her the sequence of events that led to this moment.

How did it get there?

The question was playing over and over again in my mind, repeating and analyzing the possible facts until I was near bonkers.

***

"Jacqueline."

I almost jumped out of my skin when I felt someone touch me. I looked around and realized I was still in the therapist's office, and she was staring at me curiously.

"Did you hear what I just said, Jacqueline?" she asked me.

"Well, you were talking about me."

I tried to wrap my head around what we had been talking about earlier. Truth is, I don't even remember any question I had answered.

"Yes, we were," Mrs. Gilbert smiled. "Is there anything bothering you, Jacqueline?"

I nodded almost immediately. I didn't care anymore if I would be locked up by spilling it, I just needed to get it out of my head.

"I think there's a ghost around," I said.

"What makes you think so?" she asked, looking interested and scribbling in her note pad.

"I see things, hear things," I said, remembering all the events that had occurred. It could not be coincidental that it all happened after my sister's death. The more I tried to formulate the truth in its existence, the more I felt lightheaded. The whole existence of ghosts was just too unreal to be true, and it seemed too heavy a piece of information for my brain to process all at once, yet it all seemed quite real to me.

"I dream of things, too," I continued. "Scary things. About Sandra."

"Can you tell me more about these dreams?" the therapist asked.

"She's telling me she didn't die, that I should help her."

Could it really all be connected? Was this Sandra's way of showing it to me since I took it as a mere nightmare?

"She's screaming it sometimes. And her diary…"

I suddenly felt very cold and fear washed over me. Mrs. Gilbert stood and filled a plastic cup with water. She handed it to me, and I gulped it all down at once. My hand was shaking terribly when I handed it back to her, and she gave me a few minutes to calm down, taking me through some breathing exercises until my breathing was stable again. I closed my eyes for a while as the first knock of a light headache began after a night of barely catching a wink of sleep.

"Her diary was empty," I continued, this time expressing my thoughts slow and steady. "Then a date appeared, and then she wrote something. She wrote, 'Jacky, help me'."

I visibly shook as I narrated the whole story. Mrs. Gilbert was looking at me, her blank expression not giving away her thoughts.

"Did you open the diary today?" she asked.

I shook my head. I had stayed in the living room all night, pretending to watch *Riverdale* all over again, but in truth, every other sound around me was drowned out by my shock. My mother had come down to get a glass of water, and when she tapped my shoulder, I sprung up like a frightened cat.

"What's wrong?" she asked me.

When she saw me as white as a sheet of paper, she came to hug me. I didn't say a word, but she stayed up with me. She was probably thinking I was uncomfortable with being back home after a fun weekend, but little did she know it was far from that.

"I didn't open it," I said.

I was too afraid to return to my room even though my mother had taken the diary away. She had even brought me my clothes in the morning, taking it upon herself to choose something other than black, and a very satisfied smile drew across her lips when I wore the knee-length pink dress (that used to be my favorite) without any protests. She even tied up my hair with a pink ribbon. All the while, I was still in shock, and that was how I went to school. Christy was the happiest to see me in something other than the depressing color black. My shock temporarily wore off and Sarah found it a perfect time to take a selfie with us three. She probably tagged us and added the hashtag, #ByeByeto-SadJacqueline.

After school, I insisted on going straight to my therapist's office even if it was just to wait in the reception area. My father looked pleased and my mother was trying hard to hide her smile. This was progress for both of them, seeing how their daughter was so eager to get "okay," and Dad blessed me with a kiss on my forehead after promising to pick me up afterward.

"And you believe Sandra's ghost must have written it?" Mrs. Gilbert asked.

"Well, don't you?" I threw back at her instead. "What's your psychological mumbo-jumbo for that?"

Realizing that might have sounded rude, I quickly said, "I mean, what's the psychological term for that?"

Mrs. Gilbert wrote a few things down in her note pad, something maybe like, "*Believes in ghosts and appearing messages in the writing of her dead sister, definitely needs to be chained and locked up before it gets any worse.*"

"The sensed presence," she said as soon as the pen stopped moving in her hand.

"Sensed presence?"

"The psychological mumbo-jumbo for that," she smiled. "It's called the sensed presence. It usually occurs mostly to people who have been in extreme isolation. They begin to see what is assumed to be ghosts and other presences. In your case, it's normal to have it."

"Normal?"

"Yes. It's because you are still grieving from your sister's death. You two were very close, so much so, to the point that you had a huge level of dependence on her. As a result of your grief, you've shut down, you don't socialize anymore, and your room has become your sanctuary, if I may put it that way."

I nodded slowly and waited for her to go on.

"The problem is that your stress level is high, and coupled with your constant isolation, your sensory stimulation is unchanged and leads you to trigger the presence of your lost one." She adjusted her glasses and crossed her legs. "It's a healthy coping mechanism and a normal part of the grieving process. Give it time. Also, spend less time at home and more time with your friends. Stay over at Christy's or Sarah's."

"And the writing? The one in the diary? Is it the sensed presence that wrote that as well?"

Mrs. Gilbert looked at her notes before she spoke.

"I know it can be very hard to convince you that it's all not what you make it out to be," she said. "But under psychology, there are three possibilities that can explain that."

"And they are?"

"It could be that you believe it happened, when, in truth, nothing happened," she answered.

I shook my head vehemently. I knew what I saw. I was blessed with very good eyesight and I know that dairy was on my table when I got back. If I was the only one who saw it, I would have believed it. But my mother touched it and carried it, so I was definitely not hallucinating.

"It could also be you are fabricating the story," she stated the second possibility.

"Why would I do that?" I asked incredulously.

"Just a possibility," Mrs. Gilbert said again. "We should talk more about this in the next session and you should try getting out of the house…"

"Wait, wait, wait," I stopped her. "That's two possibilities. What's the last one?"

Mrs. Gilbert took her time. I began thinking she was trying to let the time drag on so she'd not have to say it, but we had five minutes until the end of the session, and I was going nowhere until I heard all the possibilities. Even if I had to sit there all day, I would, just to make sure this had nothing to do with ghosts and everything to do with psychology.

Psychology does not find books and drop them into your house when you're not around, does it?

"Lastly, it could be it really happened just as you said," she said, causing my blood to go cold and my stomach to knot uncomfortably.

Mrs. Gilbert spoke to my Dad after the session, and I could make out words like" more vacation" and "less isolation," from where I sat in the reception area. Therapy today seemed to worsen my situation ten times more, and now I pinched myself hard on my thighs to wake up hoping this was all just a dream.

Ghosts do not exist. Sandra is dead. Ghosts do not exist. Sandra is…

Chapter 14

"Hey, dear," My father stopped the mantra I was playing over and over in my head. "Let's go and get some frozen yogurt, shall we?"

I got up from my seat and followed after him to the car. My obedient and unreluctantly brand-new self sat well with my parents, especially my mother, and they did not look worried as to whether or not something must be wrong with me to change overnight. Suddenly, the pink I was wearing disgusted me and my senses were returning from my shocked state already.

"Let's go shopping instead," I suggested.

"Shopping? Okay, then." My Dad took the next turn and headed towards the mall. The weather was hot, and summer brought a liquid kind of humidity that you only feel in our part of the south. Today, Sarah swore she fried an egg on her mother's car hood from the scorching heat of the sun. I had asked her how it tasted, and she looked at me and laughed. I told her I was curious as to whether Mother Nature was any good as a cook.

The mall was as full as any other day. My father handed me his card and followed me as I stepped into the crowded place. It was strange going shopping with Dad for the first time, and stranger going without my sister who had been blessed with a great taste in fashion, more like a special talent she possessed. I didn't want to waste any time trying on clothes and posing for my Dad's opinion only to be showered with the exaggerated compliments he tossed out just to make me happy, when, in truth, it made things embarrassing in front of the shop attendants.

I went to the usual shop my sister and I used to go to. I picked out anything black and paid for them at the counter and my Dad's expression was that of a very worried man.

"Honey, are you sure you don't want to choose other colors? Summer in Alabama just doesn't scream black clothing."

"Nope."

"Something like..." He walked away and brought a white top that looked like an artist had vomited paint on it and called it a design. "This?"

I shook my head. "Nope."

He held up a floral dress that I would rather go naked than wear in public. "What about this pretty sundress."

I shook my head again. "Still a no."

My father tried with other clothes, but I rejected every one of them. Giving up, he drove us back home, only to be met by my mother standing at the porch and waving at us. She was wearing an apron, and it was rare to see her back from work so early. She didn't do much at work since she partnered with one of her friends to run a private elementary school. It was basically her being in an office and checking on the children's welfare.

"You went shopping! Aww!" She cooed at me like I was a puppy. "Let's see what you've got there, Darlin'."

She took the bag from my hand and carried it in while I slumped myself down on the living room couch waiting for the anger to erupt after seeing my shopping bag contents.

"Jacqueline! Seriously?"

I hid a smile and turned to look at her. She was holding up my clothes for me, and I feigned confusion at her question.

"What did I do wrong?"

She dumped the clothes on the seat next to me and sat by my side, taking my hands in hers. She squeezed, perhaps meaning it to be an affectionate one, but there was an angry grip like iron.

"How many people loved what you wore today and told you how much better you looked in that outfit?" she asked.

I shrugged. "I wasn't counting or listening."

"You see? There were just so many you lost count!"

My mother smiled, and behind that smile was a patience she was trying so hard not to break.

"How about this? Let's return all these tomorrow and we'll do some proper shopping together, huh? Just us girls."

I shrugged again, and she took that as a yes, because she was back to being the preppy woman who greeted us at the doorstep. She kissed my cheeks and stood, returning to her work in the kitchen. The dining room table looked like she was preparing a buffet for guests, and I was allergic to guests.

"I'm going to go and visit Christy," I said.

"What? No. Mr. and Mrs. Foster are coming over for dinner and I want you to see them."

She smiled and broke two eggs together inside a bowl. The minute I heard those names, I knew I had to escape before it was too late. The said couple had a bad habit of pinching my cheeks ever since I was ten and complimenting my parents on how well fed I was, like I was a farm pig waiting for slaughter. Even though I was far from the chubby kid I was two years ago, they still found joy in doing that. They had triplets, annoying five-year-old boys with voices too loud for their ages, and I preferred my ears to function properly.

"Yeah, well, the therapist said I should go out more so I won't commit suicide," I told my mother. Low blow, but worth it.

My mother unconsciously slapped two more eggs together and the contents plus the shells dropped into the bowl.

"What?!"

My father, who was busy flipping TV, spoke. "Mrs. Gilbert said the house is suffocating for her and she needs to be out as much as she can."

I exchanged glances with my father and caught the smile on his lips and a wink of his eye. I planned to text him about how much I loved him later.

"Oh, dear God," My mother was by my side again at once, wrapping me in a tight embrace. "Dear God, is it really that hard for you, Jacqueline?"

Guilt surfaced, but the determination to avoid those guests overcame that guilt as I nodded in affirmation and my mother gasped.

"I'm really sorry," she said. "You can go on to Christy's and stay over if you like. Okay? I'll pay for therapy 'til you get okay, I promise you."

I wanted to tell her it was not just therapy that mattered, but home as well. I wanted to return to a being a family, just the way we used to be before, except I wanted to be loved this time. Before I went, I changed into a pair of ripped jeans and a top from my newly-purchased clothes and my mother did not try to make me change. She stopped me before I went out and gave me a long kiss on my forehead. It was annoying to me because I could see the pity seeping in through her actions and I hate pity.

Chapter 15

Christy was reading when I went up to her room. She sat on her bed with a large textbook open before her. I watched her for a while, cheek resting against her raised knee, glasses on, hair as messy as her room. She was lost in concentration. I ran in and jumped on her bed, causing her to startle and scream.

"Jacqueline!" she reprimanded lightly.

"Missed you, too," I laughed, putting my face directly in front of her face. She hit me with a pillow and closed the book shut, giving me her full attention.

"I didn't know you were coming over," she said.

"I didn't know I was bringing myself over."

I sat up. "The Fosters are coming for dinner at my house."

"Oh," She said, realizing my reason for bailing out and coming to her house. "And how did you escape your mother?"

I didn't tell her about my therapy sessions and the leverage I had over my parents now that I was one step from going to crazy town, so I just smiled mischievously instead. I had no plans of ever telling her because Christy was already being extra super nice. I didn't need her being even nicer to me just because her best friend was seeing a shrink. That was not something I could bear.

"You sneaky little snake," Christy nudged me. "You're safe here."

She went back to her reading and I was back to my brooding. The thing I loved about Christy was that she understood me, sometimes maybe more than I understood myself. When she saw I was in no mood to chat, she let me be and never took any offense. My mind drifted back to where it had been for every hour of the day, to the glittery diary that found its way back to my room. The therapist had asked if I'd opened it, and now I had a feeling I should have done that. If that diary was some method of communication between Sandra and me, I should not ignore it. I needed to be brave enough to open it and talk to her.

If I was going to do this crazy thing, I had to do so before the dark skies of the night fully descended. I didn't have the guts to open that book in darkness. The sky was already the color of sunset orange, so I had to hurry back.

"I'm going back," I told Christy and hopped to my feet.

"Oh, come on, let's spend the night together," she pleaded. Her phone rang and she asked me to wait while she answered it. It was Sarah on the other end, and I waited impatiently while they talked.

"Sarah is asking if we can come for a study night at her place," Christy said loudly, waiting for me to answer.

I shook my head in the negative, "Can't."

"Oh." Christy's excitement descended into disappointment. "Well, I'll tell her then. Maybe tomorrow night," she said, with a hopeful lilt in her voice.

I left before she ended the call, and just as I said my goodnights to Christy's parents and opened the front door to make my swift exit, I met face to face with the devil incarnate. He was just coming from football practice, and he looked like he needed a serious bath from the sweat that drenched his entire body.

A corner of his lips lifted up in a smirk. "Hey, Wednesday."

I returned a tight-lipped smile back at him, not ready for snarky comments and comebacks. He blocked my way before I could walk past him.

"Wow, nothing from you?" He feigned surprise. "Cat got your tongue or something?"

"You'll be losing yours if you don't let me pass," I retorted.

Eric gave me a million-dollar smile like I had just told him he had gotten into the college of his dreams.

"Now that's the Dracula I know," he commented. "Listen, Jacqueline, there's something I need to tell you."

I paused. He had called me by my name and not some dark movie villain. And to top that, he was actually looking serious. That meant he may have wanted to say something sensible from his mouth. This was new and definitely worth hearing.

"I know I've been such a... *not so nice* guy sometimes," I scoffed at his description of himself. "But I want us to be friends now. What do you say?"

"I say how much did you have to drink?"

Eric laughed. He stretched out both arms like a tightrope walker on an invisible rope and walked in a straight line from the stairs then across the road and back just to prove he was not the least bit inebriated.

"None," he stated after walking back to me. "Whatcha say? Truce?"

There was a nagging feeling that he had a trick up his sleeves. Even though he seemed sincere, something didn't feel right, like it was not a complete one-hundred percent. How could he wake up one morning after years of torturing me and suddenly decide to put an end to all his shenanigans? If life worked that way, bullying would have ceased to exist a long time ago.

"I'll think about it," I said.

"Come on, Jacqueline," he used my real name again and it sounded strange hearing it from his mouth. He pouted and slouched his shoulders. "Okay, just give me a hug and let's forget this."

That was where I got it. He just wanted to infect me with his germs and get his sweat on me. It was all a boorish act! Could he get any more disgusting?

"If you come any closer…" I warned.

"You'll cut my tongue out?" He laughed. "Get in here."

I screamed as he engulfed me in a hug of woody cologne mixed with sweet pungent sweat. It was a horrible smell, and when he released me after about two full minutes, my clothes and body smelt just like him. If I were a boy, I'd have taken off my shirt and walked home shirtless, but I was a girl, and the world would not appreciate me baring my blooming body for all to see. So, I was going to be stuck with his stench until I got home.

I would have rather taken a bath in Shrek's swamp.

"I hate you, Eric Edgewood!" I screeched.

"Ah." Yup, there it was, he was satisfied. "Those three little words made my day. G'night, Ninja."

He was still chuckling victoriously as he stepped past me and into the house. I had to run all the way back home to get his smell off my body as fast as I could and burn my clothes.

Maybe not burn the clothes. They were too nice and expensive to dispose of so easily.

If cooties existed, I would have been infected by now. Eric himself was a walking virus. Eric had been a pain in my behind for as long as I could remember, and he always chased me around when I was little, knowing I feared cooties when my immature self thought they existed. I believed he was created specifically to make my life hell, and nothing was ever enough for him, *ever*. Cooties might have existed back in the olden days and were not some made up story to keep boys and girls away from each other. Well, who knows, since ghosts most likely do exist.

THE ROSE DIARY

Chapter 16

When I entered the house, there were loud greetings gushing out like I was a child celeb or something, and that was followed by the familiar ear-piercing noise of the three gnomes. Mrs. Foster was the first to stand, then her husband. They were both approaching me, zoning in on my face which was easily prone to acne since my entry into the near teenage years, so definitely a no-touch zone.

"Please, don't!" My voice was surprisingly firm.

They stopped. Mr. Foster stood up straight while Mrs. Foster's arms were still curved, poised for a hug, but frozen in mid-effort.

"You're so cute," she unfroze and continued her approach, and just before her fingers could touch my face, I took hold of both her hands in mine, shook them vigorously, and prevented the contact with my pre-teen acne.

"I really don't like it when both of you pinch my cheeks." I told them. "You've got three little kids blessed with all the cheek fat you can pinch and pinch and pinch 'til it deflates. I've lost mine already."

Both Mr. and Mrs. Foster blinked blankly, surprised at my words, but I'd had enough already. I could literally feel my mother's barely-concealed glare piercing the back of my head as I ascended the stairs. I'd eventually get away from it since I was the suicidal one. Well, at least to her knowledge.

I marched up to my room with intentional stomps on the stairs to wash off the horrid smell. I stopped short when I saw the door to my sister's room was once again open. Fear crept into me and chilled me to my bones, but I forced my legs to step into the room. It was still neat, untouched, no sign of any ghost lounging on the bed or using any of her stuff. Did they use any technology over in the afterworld?

The sparkle of something shiny got caught in my peripheral view. It was the glittery diary staring right back at me. It was on top of her stack of books, and the fear that overcame me as I approached it was freezingly mind-numbing. Outside the window, I saw that the Foster brood was already leaving, and I knew it would not be long until my name would ring in the four corners of this house from the angry mouth of my mother, so I had to hurry.

Sucking in a slow deep breath, I picked up the dairy. I opened to the first page and it still held the same message. I flipped over to the second page and there, staring boldly at me was another message with today's date on it.

'Don't be scared, Jacky. I need your help and you're the only one who can help me. '

The diary dropped from my hands that were now shaking like I was having a seizure. A cold sweat broke out, and I backed away from the book.

"It can't be true." I said. "It… it can't be true. It's all in my head. It's all in my head. Sandra is dead. Ghosts do not exist. Sandra is dead. Ghosts…"

"Do exist," a voice behind me whispered.

When I turned to look back, my vocal cords must have burst from the scream that rang from my mouth, and everything went dark.

Chapter 17

My mother once fainted right before my eyes.
Sandra and I were in the kitchen talking about who was the most handsome one of the Jonas brothers and my mother had supported Sandra's belief that Nick Jonas should win the trophy for best-looking in the whole music industry. I rooted for Joe Jonas, and my reason was that his voice held so much more depth and such depth can only come from a soul filled with emotions.

"After all, like they say, beauty is only skin deep," I said.

Sandra was surprised by my answer, and she said it was strange hearing such a poetic answer from someone my age. I was the one who caught a glimpse of Mom staggering when she opened the fridge, but she abated my worries when she gave me a reassuring smile. I continued talking with Sandra, now moving on to the topic of The Kardashians. I never understood anything about why they broadcasted their lives on TV. I mean, I for one would prefer to live in a cave than be that exposed and here were these crazy people calling attention to themselves even when they were in their supposed comfort zone. The world is a strange place.

It was a thud that drew our attention, and Mom was nowhere to be found. Sandra sprang to her feet and let out a scream at the sight of Mom's lifeless body on the floor. I remember thinking she had died, and the first thought that popped into my head was who was going to make me Nutella pancakes like she did. Sandra tried to calm me down by saying that Mom was just having a quick nap. I was smarter than that. Who just drops in the middle of the kitchen floor because they want to have a nap?

My mother was dead was all I knew.

I tried dragging her toward the living room while Sandra called 911, but her body was far too heavy for me to pull all by myself. We did manage to drag her away from the marble floor and onto the carpeted one, and from the way her head kept hitting the ground continuously, she should have had a concussion. However, when she woke up in the hospital and claimed she did not remember anything about the paramedics carrying her to the van, I believed two things:

One, she was pretending the whole time.

Two, she did actually die and came back to life. Fainting was just a very deep sleep, but not to the point you'd be completely unaware of what was happening around you.

However, my theory was proven wrong when I woke up to stark white ceilings in a very unfamiliar room. There was the sound of someone crying quietly, and I could make out the blurry figure of someone in white, and then a groan escaped my lips.

There was a gasp, and soon, my mother's hands were all over my face.

"Jacqueline! Honey!" She cried some more. "Are you okay? Are you hurt? Tell me..."

"She's fine," the man in white coat spoke. My father pried my mother away from me, looking just as worried as she, only he was less dramatic.

"How do you feel?" he asked me.

I sat up and hissed when an ache slashed through my head. The man in the white coat, which I assumed was a doctor, gently pushed me back to recline against my pillow. My throat felt as dry as the Sahara, and when I tried to request a cup of water, a terrible pain was all I could produce. I closed my eyes and held on to my throat. The doctor himself took the cup of water from the dispenser and handed it to me.

"You strained them," he explained. "Your vocal cords. But don't worry, they'll heal soon, and you'll be talking normally. But for now, minimize your speech as much as you can, okay? I'll also administer some drugs."

He continued talking to my parents about more medical stuff, and I massaged the painful throb. The nurse came in and gave me a shot of something and I started to feel eerily calm. My muscles relaxed and the pain was giving way to a nice floaty feeling.

"But what made her scream and faint?" I heard my mother say, but as if she was far away. She looked down at me and asked, "Jacqueline, what made you so scared?"

Sandra had been there. Well, it was not exactly her but an image of her floating lightly and reaching out to me. There was no warning beforehand, not even some sort of note like, *'I'm appearing in a second and I'm gonna scare the living daylights out of you.'* It felt like a dream, but there was enough proof of me waking up other than somewhere in my bedroom and being temporarily mute, and nothing was stronger evidence than my mother's cries.

"The diary," I mumbled. "Sandra... writing words, help," slowly, I slid into a deep, comfortable sleep.

I was discharged that very same day, and the thought of going back to that house straight from the hospital was more than I could bear. My mother thought I needed some support since my state of mind was *breakable*, so she held tightly to my hand as we three made our way to the car. I took out my phone, typed my message on it, and showed my mother.

"You want to stay at Christy's?" my mother asked.

"But, Darling," my father spoke. "You've only just gotten discharged. You need proper attention."

"I want to stay there," I croaked painfully. My mother shushed me in an instant, saying something about my role in the Drama Club and ending my future acting career if I strain what was left of my voice. Not that it mattered anyway; I sucked at acting.

I finally got my way and we headed over to Christy's. My parents sat and spoke with Christy's parents. Christy looked at me as we sat at the kitchen isle, her eyes watery. She put a hand to my throat and massaged lightly, and her eyes got sadder when I didn't react to that.

"Does it hurt really bad?" she asked. Deciding it was tiresome to explain via text, I just nodded. She gave me support by hugging me, and that was when her demon-possessed brother walked in, ignoring us and waltzing to the fridge, his ears encased in a pair of headphones. He took the milk bottle and guzzled milk right from it, two trails forming by the sides of his mouth. Christy made an irritated sound.

"I'm telling Mom!" she yelled at him.

"Snitch." He glared back at her and drank more milk like a thirsty pig before returning the bottle back to the fridge. That got me thinking about all the milk I'd drank over at Christy's and how it must have been infected with the germs of this quasi-human related to her. *I bet he ate out of peanut butter and jelly jars with his hands too; how disgusting*, I thought.

"Hey, Vulture," he greeted me, making wild gesticulatory signs like he was speaking to a deaf and dumb person.

"Heeelllooo," he flapped his arms, trying harder to get my attention. How I wish I could have recorded him and showed him how utterly stupid he looked. "How does it feel to be *special*?"

"She's not deaf, doofus." Christy chucked a spoon at him and missed. "Just leave her alone."

"Oh, poor Vulture," he pouted, then laughed, placing his headphones back on his head and dancing around like the complete fool he was. Christy sighed and apologized as if her brother's actions were her responsibility. My parents came to join us, telling Christy to take good care of me and giving me the dreaded news that I would be skipping school the next day, so I would be able to rest properly. I wanted to tell them resting would make no difference for my voice, but even when I attempted to speak, the pain cut sharply in my throat, leaving me with no choice other than to remain the mute girl while they made rules. They told Christy not to talk to me. They both kissed me goodbye, and after they left, I went up to Christy's room and laid down on her bed. Christy kept to her promise and we stayed together in the silence of boredom, with her stealing glances at me. She kept biting her lip like she was about to say something, but eventually, we both dozed off only waking up for dinner then returning to her room and back to sleep again.

My mother was at the door to pick me up the very next morning. She did not even wait for me to have breakfast claiming she could not sleep all night because she was worried about me. I followed her *wordlessly*, waved at Christy *wordlessly*, and walked down to our place *wordlessly*. Dad was at the dining table still in his robe, reading a newspaper and chewing noisily on his cereal.

"Hey, Jacqueline," he greeted me, his cheer as cringe-worthy as the birds that sang completely out-of-tune outside the windows. I was beginning to wonder if I was running away from the ghosts or from the overly and unusual affectionate behavior of my parents. Maybe if Sandra's ghost could appear before them, then perhaps the attention would be off me and back onto her again.

Well, if that ever happened, we would certainly need a family therapy session and I cannot imagine that happening.

Mom was making Nutella-stuffed pancakes, part of the uncomfortable attention thing they had going in an effort to do things that pleased me since my mental state had gone south. Mom hummed as she whisked, smiling at me when I stared blankly at her while Dad's noisy eating filled the silence. My eyes drifted towards the stairs, and there was the chill of the North Pole freezing my bones as I remembered what had happened the day before.

Mom was talking with Dad now, asking if the Doctor had checked to make sure I didn't have any internal bleeding of any sort. Dad said it was their job to do so, and Mom said the thud I made with my head was enough to hammer a nail into the wall.

Well, not her words exactly, but something like that. Once again, it was like I wasn't there, and truth be told, I mostly wasn't. Most of me was upstairs waiting for more messages from my dead sister.

They both concluded they should take me for another checkup. Another day planned, and another decision made without me adding a single opinion of my own. A plate of fluffy pancakes was thrust toward me. Mom pressed her lips to my forehead as she placed a knife and fork in my hands. I was expecting a baby bib to be set around my neck as well, and when that was not forthcoming, well… I dug into my meal. Mom practically hovered over me like a helicopter waiting for a place to land, making sure I ate every bite. She kept encouraging like a toddler who was learning to eat for the first time and I'm sure I made her extremely proud when I finished every bite.

The worst happened when both of them told me they were taking a day off from work as well. That was when I knew I had had enough, and it was either upstairs with Sandra's ghost or downstairs with the torment of their sickly-sweet behavior. I opened my mouth to speak, and my mother quickly put a finger to my lip to silence me.

"Type it out, Darling," she said. I took my phone and typed out that I was going to sleep, and she nodded.

"Alright, let me…"

I swear, if she was going to say tuck me into bed, I was going to lose it.

"…tuck you in."

"I can do just fine," I coughed as I spoke, the words squeezing out painfully. "Can you guys just please leave me alone? I just lost my voice. I'm not dying, and…"

"Jacqueline, Jacqueline." My mother shushed me. "We get it, no need to strain yourself. Go on upstairs."

My father did not say anything, thankfully, so I stomped my way up the stairs, my legs feeling like heavy logs of wood refusing to be lifted up.

Instead of heading straight to my room, I went to open Sandra's bedroom door without any second thoughts, and much to my relief and dismay, it was locked. Definitely Mom. If Sandra wanted to talk to me, maybe I should allow her to, and I needed her diary to help me do that for I had no skills in summoning ghosts.

Too bad Hogwarts was fictional.

I went into my room and searched everywhere for the diary, but I couldn't find it. I was fully hoping Sandra would have dropped it for me, but it was nowhere to be found. Frustrated, I sat on my bed, almost laughing out loud at myself. Yesterday, I fainted at the sight of a ghost and today I was anticipating a conversation with one; *how much crazier can I get?*

Chapter 18

I was laying on my bed texting with Christy while she ate lunch and she told me she was eating alone in the cafeteria. The reason was Sarah was eating her lunch with Caramel instead, leaving poor, sweet Christy all alone. I was not the least bit surprised. I had always expected the hot Sarah Jennings would eventually join Caramel's 'gang' instead of hanging around with us. Let's face it, she had the beauty and the fashion and could have even overthrown Caramel after a while.

I talked with Christy throughout lunch, via messages of course, since I couldn't whisper without Mama Bear being there in a second. Sleep came out of boredom, and even my nap was dreamless; it was almost as if nothing happened. There was no sign of my sister, the diary was locked up in her room, and asking Mom for the key was totally impossible.

Mom came up when I was busy reading a novel, deciding to put my overload of free time to good use. She placed a cup of hot chocolate on my bedside table, then closed my book and tilted my chin up to look at her. She did not say anything for a while, then brushed her fingers through my hair, and a sigh left her lips.

"Is it really very hard for you, Jacqueline?" she asked softly. "Your sister's... demise, is it really very hard on you?"

I looked away and continued reading my book. She wanted a heart-to-heart now, next thing we'd be braiding each other's hair's while swapping secrets.

"Jacqueline!" she said sharply, and I put down my book.

"You can just write it out, here." She gave me a pen and a note that I did not know she was holding. "Just write it out."

I stared at the blank page, and even the space there was too little to pour out the garbage of emotions and junk of words from my head. I wanted to tell her how she and Dad were suffocating me with their terrible terms of endearment and their constant hovering around me. I wanted to tell her that I was human as well, and my feelings mattered no matter how much they claimed to" want the best for me." Every time they made decisions for me like I was an invisible doll that had no idea how life worked it disturbed me. I wanted to tell her to allow me to make mistakes like every normal human and learn from them instead of straightening me out with harsh tones and "I told you so's." I could feel Mom's eyes on me as I held up the pen, and then I wrote what I just wanted in that moment and handed it back to her.

Her face fell.

"Okay then, I'll leave you alone, dear," she said. She pressed another kiss against my forehead and stood, closing the door after her. Knowing that even that would not keep her away and needing a breath of fresh air, I stepped out after her, jogged down the stairs and opened the front door.

"Are you going for a walk, dear?" my father asked, and I nodded just before I shut the door. The welcoming softness of the evening greeted me, and as I walked down the street, a certain kind of calm descended upon me. The sun was making a grand exit far off in the sky, casting its golden glow on the clouds and creating a masterpiece with swirls of orange and pink. Some high-school girls were approaching in the opposite direction, probably heading home from extra classes or detention. They were giggling at a high pitch to look 'attractive' and I started to walk past them, but one of them stopped me.

"Hey," she said. I looked at her, brushing away my hair from my face to give her a proper perusal thinking she had probably mistaken me for someone else.

"I think we've met before," she said. I was uncomfortable, casting glances at the curious looks her friends gave me. She must have noticed because she told them she would meet up with them later.

"I'm Diana," she stretched out a hand. This Diana girl was a tall, plain-looking teenager with short brown hair and an easy smile. She continued to smile even when I didn't accept the handshake. Instead, she tucked her hands into the back pockets of her shorts.

"Listen, I was hoping we would meet again someday." She brought out a thin bracelet from her tote bag and my eyes widened. It was the birthday gift Sandra had given me on my twelfth birthday, the very last one she'd ever celebrate with me. It was customized with my nickname. I'd forgotten about it and the last time I remember having it on was...

It clicked in my head. That night I ran out of the house. That night some teenagers from a party stopped and one hugged me until my parents came...

Was she...?

"I found it after you left." She took my hand and dropped the bracelet into it. "Figured you'd want that back. It's really beautiful, by the way."

I nodded absent-mindedly and stared at the piece of silver in my hand. I was not a huge fan of emotions, but something welled up in me, something that felt like gratitude and happiness.

"Thank you." I said, despite my hoarse voice. "Thank you very much."

Diana smiled, standing there like she wanted to say more, but didn't. Then she waved a little gesture of goodbye at me and ran ahead to meet her friends. She could have just chosen to pawn it and get a decent amount of money for it, but it seemed the world was not all selfish and dark after all. I fixed the bracelet on my wrist, and I was sure if my sister's ghost was lurking around somewhere, she would be smiling as well. Or could it be that Diana was sent to deliver this to me?

I looked over at Diana's retreating back and the question kept bugging me. I shook my head, trying to rid it of the possibility and continued my walk, this time my feet lighter and infected by the easy smile of my bracelet rescuer.

The sun had made an exit when I returned back home, and I saw the worried look on my mother's face as she paced the kitchen floor. She looked at me, relief in her eyes, but said nothing. My father also said nothing, throwing me just a "Welcome back" and returned his eyes to the television. Mom was making dinner, but I was nowhere close to hungry, so I decided to skip it and have an early night. I wanted the day to end as quickly as possible.

Chapter 19

Deep into the night, a dream made me bolt up from sleep. My breaths were coming out in rapid gasps and my entire body was sweaty. The horror of the dream was still fresh in my head. Tears trickled down my face and I covered my mouth to shut up the screams that almost made their way out of my throat. I grabbed my phone lying by the bedside table. The time read 2:43 a.m., and I dialed Christy's number.

She did not pick up on the first two rings, and now the tears were falling like a waterfall down my cheeks. I was getting frantic. I needed someone to talk to me before lost it completely.

She picked up on the third try.

"Christy..." I was crying and my throat felt flooded with emotions and the pain of my vocal cords. I gulped for air so I could not drown from it all. "Christy, it was so horrible, she... blood... Sandra... Christy."

I was weeping uncontrollably now, and when my name was called, I stopped short, because the person on the other end did not sound the least bit like my friend.

"Hello?" I called again to be sure. "Christy? You there?"

"Christy's asleep." The person I dreaded most in this world answered. "I could hear her phone all the way from my room. I don't know who still listens to Justin Bieber these days."

"Oh." I said with a sniffle, wiping away the snot from my nose.

"She usually leaves it on vibrate though," he said. I could hear a tired yawn from him. Maybe she left it in the hope that I would call.

So much for light sleeping.

"I guess... just tell her I called and... I'm sorry for disturbing..." I stuttered, feeling very embarrassed that he had heard me in my moment of complete vulnerability.

"Do you always get such bad dreams?" he asked.

"What?"

"The nightmares," he said. He was unbelievably calm and unlike the idiotic Eric that terrorized my very existence. It was very unreal, as unreal as ghosts and diaries that wrote themselves.

"I've always had them, but I guess they got more pronounced after…" I gulped audibly. "After it all."

There was no reply from the other side, and I thought he must have dropped the phone somewhere while I spoke. I was wrong, however, and suddenly he spoke again.

"Christy has nightmares once in a while too," he said. "And I tell her, as long as there is someone by your side, you've got nothing to worry about."

His words made fresh tears trickle down my face. I really missed Sandra. It ached my heart to the point I was feeling the pain physically.

"It's okay, Jacqueline," he said softly. "You've got all of us, so it's okay."

I nodded, despite the fact that he couldn't see me, then I hiccupped, let out a loud cry, and the tears would not cease to come.

"Christy says a song calms her down," he said. "Would you like me to sing you one?"

Without hesitation, I nodded, then realizing again that he couldn't see me, I said, "Yes, please."

He started out slowly, lyrics of a song unfamiliar to me. Truth be told, his voice was not good; it was amazing. I laid down with the phone pressed to my ear, listening as his voice carried away the fear and anxiety from my heart and the wells of my tears closed up. If Sandra was alive and I told her that her crush had sung me a song to lull me to sleep on my most terrifying of nights, I wonder how surprised she would be. And when she would ask what it sounded like, if it was anything like Nick Jonas' or Joe Jonas', I would have shaken my head and told her it was simply one thing.

Heavenly.

Chapter 20

There was a story my mother told us at bedtime when Sandra and I were younger.

It was a story about a little girl and her mother. The little girl had two apples in her hands, and her mother had requested sweetly to have one of the apples. The little girl took a bite from both apples, leaving the mother disappointed and probably wondering, 'Where did I go wrong in raising this girl?' However, the next action of her daughter took her by surprise, and she handed one of the apples to her mother and said,

"Take this one, Mommy. This is the sweeter one."

That story was one of my very first lessons about not being judgmental of people and learning that people are not always as they seem to be. Their surface might be covered in slime and goo, but their insides were built from polished gold.

I wondered if the same thing applied to Eric when I sat at the cafeteria two days later, munching on a cold fry as Christy focused on her burger. The burger tasted like a piece of tasteless flattened meat and stale bread, but Christy had one rule; as long as it can fill you up and it was not poison, you eat as much as you can to avoid starving.

"Hey, you eating that?" Christy asked, dusting off specks of crumbs from her mouth. I shook my head and pushed the tray towards her, and she was about to dig in, but stopped.

"I'm sorry, I should not have asked," she said, pushing the tray back to me. "You've barely eaten anything."

"Well, that's because it tastes like trash." My voice was getting better and the pain in my throat was subsiding. At least it did not feel like I ate a cactus any more.

"At least finish your fries," Christy urged.

I ate a couple more fries, dropped my leftovers in front of my hungry pal, picked up my tray and stood.

Christy smiled and dug into my meal in a hot second. My eyes trailed over to Sarah who was seated close to Caramel at the 'Divas' table located at the center of the hall where they could bathe in attention. She was laughing with them, a sound very unlike her usual bubbly laughter. She twirled a strand of her hair when Caramel twirled a strand of her hair and joined their synchronization of cackles when what they hoped was a joke was cracked and shoved meals around their plates the whole time to avoid getting more calories into their skinny frames.

Sarah was laughing, throwing her head back when she caught my stare. She gave me a pointed look and turned away. I tore my gaze away from her and back to the hungry lion cub almost done with my meal. I was aching to ask her if Eric had told her anything about the night I called, but Christy would have told me over lunch, so that meant he had kept it from her.

"Did you fast or something?" I asked her when she was licking up the ketchup.

"I get crazy hungry these days," she confessed, throwing out a loud belch all of a sudden. Her eyes widened in surprise, and we both giggled.

"And I am trying to eat enough to not die," I said. Christy stopped licking the ketchup and looked over at me with her sad eyes.

"You know, if it's the food, you can always go to Aunt Margaret's on weekends," she said.

"And ransack her fridge?"

"And her pantry, and her cookbook!" she added, and we both laughed. It was when I looked away that I caught Sarah eyeing us, and for that brief millisecond, it almost looked like she was smiling, too.

The thought of telling Christy about my encounter with a ghost crossed my mind, but I brushed it off. So far, I had not seen anything weird in the last few days, so safe to say, maybe it would not ever happen again.

But then I remembered the messages in the diary, and deep inside of me, I felt that I had not seen the last of her. However, his time, I knew I would not burst my vocal cords. I was prepared, to say the least, and I wanted to know why all this was happening to me, and the meaning behind those messages.

"Wanna come over to my place?" Christy asked, throwing the textbook into her bag when the final school bell rang.

"How about we do not head home directly?" I suggested. "My parents are thinking I want your parents to adopt me."

"Well, it's not such a bad idea. I'll be more than glad to have you as a sister," she laughed. I was about to say something along the lines of not wanting to be related to her devil of a brother but stopped myself short. Ever since he had unearthed a part of himself that I didn't know existed, it felt wrong to insult him.

"How about we get some popsicles?" Christy beamed.

"What are you, five?"

"It would be so nice to be five again," she said. "So, we're getting popsicles. Come on."

Christy was talking about which flavor she would like when I saw Sarah standing on the stairs looking like she was waiting for someone. I told Christy we should go and talk to her, but Christy refused, saying she did not want anyone to ruin her mood.

"You cannot force someone to be friends with you," Christy said.

"She's still our friend. She's just into being one of the cool kids right now," I replied.

I walked toward Sarah, her eyes casting an annoyed look as I approached her. She stood several inches taller than me in the cute wedges she wore.

"Hey Sarah," I greeted her.

"Hey," she replied in a monotone of feigned boredom.

"Christy and I are going to get some popsicles," I said. "Wanna come with?"

She scoffed and looked at me. "How old do I look? Five?"

"Well, I said the same thing to cat eyes over there," I pointed to Christy. "But I remembered you loved the red ones, and hey, we can all be five together."

Her facial expression softened, and she opened her mouth to speak, but as she cast her gaze sideways, Caramel and two other minions were coming up to us. Caramel gave me a sickly caramelized smile.

"Jacqueline," she purred like she was close to pouncing on me. "Sorry, you can't follow us to Sarah's. She's only inviting friends."

I looked at Sarah who had always been my friend and she dropped her chin.

"Yeah, well, I never found nail painting and gossip fun anyways," I said. "Have fun, Sarah." At that, I turned and walked away.

"And, oh Jacqueline," Caramel called me back. She waltzed towards me, stopping when we were nearly face to face and batted her lashes.

"It's high time you stopped mourning, don't you think?" She asked. "I mean, there's a whole lot of colors other than black at the mall, you know?"

I smiled at her. "I know, I just like matching that black eye I gave you. Care for another?" I said balling my right hand into a fist.

She went rigid, and she was practically seething through her nostrils, but I turned abruptly and waved triumphantly over my shoulder at them without looking back and joined Christy. Christy raised her brows in question, and I shook my head to indicate it was just the two of us having our popsicles on this fine sunny day.

After having three rounds of cold, sticky sweetness, and a mild case of brain freeze, I headed to Christy's place. Eric had football practice for the big game the following week. They were facing their rival, East High so he wouldn't be home to drive me crazy.

I sent a quick text to my parents informing them I would be home late. Christy and I got started on our homework, the fun way to spend our after-school hours. We paused on a tricky math question, each of us brainstorming on our worksheet. I heaved a sigh and looked at the bracelet clasped on my wrist. I was still trying to wrap my head around how the girl had recognized me despite it being dark that evening. I figured out it must have been the street light.

A victorious yell from Christy drew me back to the matter at hand. She had solved it, and then we moved on to the next problem.

I ate some junk food then prepared to leave. As I was walking down the hall towards the stairs, it was Eric's partially-opened door that made me stop, curiosity getting the better of me. I had never been inside his room, and it would do no harm to see what it looked like. I pushed his door a little more, craning my neck to see what was inside. There were several posters of different soccer players and some awards in a glass cupboard. I strained my eyes to see the positions for which he was awarded but couldn't read them from where I stood, so I just took in as much of his room as I could. I didn't dare go inside, but I was struck by the contrasting neatness to Christy's, the white theme and the simplicity of it.

"Seen enough?" someone asked, and I screamed. I backed away quickly, but it was too late, I had been caught.

"I… was… I didn't…" I stuttered.

"Snooping around is not something I expected of you, but well, ain't people full of surprises," he frowned. He looked worn out, his eyes tired and his hair matted flatly from all the sweat pouring from his scalp, He did not look happy, and I felt I was the sole reason.

"I was just…"

"Don't try to deny it", he scowled. "Now, can I enter my room, or would you like to check through my laptop, as well?"

I stepped out of the way and he closed the door shut. It was as if the boy that sang to me that night with softness in his voice and the boy who came in just now completely pissed off were two different people entirely. Maybe they were twins, you know, the good and the evil one, but unfortunately, I think they just cohabitated in the same body. Well, he said it: 'ain't humans full of surprises?'

I wished there was a delete button for memories like nothing ever happened.

Chapter 21

"And how are you today, Jacqueline?" Mrs. Gilbert was as cheery as ever. *The sun would be so jealous of her radiance,* I thought, trying not to hear the sarcasm in my own head.

This positive thinking stuff is actually working well for me.

"Well, I'm as happy as Eeyore to be here," I replied, and she raised a confused brow.

"Isn't Eeyore the really sad and tired donkey in *Winnie the Pooh*?"

"You betcha!"

"Hmm," was all she said and wrote in her notepad. One of these days, I would find a way to steal that notepad and read all the "wise words" she had been writing since the beginning of this therapy stuff. It was annoying how she'd write, look up at me, adjust her glasses a bit then resume writing.

What was I, some virus she was studying like in a laboratory?

"And about the diary and Sandra?" she asked.

How I wished I knew where my mother had hidden my sister's room keys. I could have asked her directly, but I knew she would not hand them over, and might even be encouraged to hide it somewhere even more difficult for me to find.

"Nothing on that," I answered.

"Do you still believe her ghost is around somewhere?"

"Yes, I do."

"Okay." She wrote some more in her note pad. I briefed her about what happened and how I had temporarily lost my voice, and she was taking notes after a pause. The more I thought about it, the less scary it all became.

"How about the nightmares?"

I shivered as I remembered the last nightmare I had.

"I saw her," I began.

"Sandra?" the therapist asked, and I nodded.

"She... she was hurt or... I don't really know." I pushed my fingers through my hair and rested my forehead in my palms. "Her body was sort of transparent, see-through…"

She was lying on her side in the middle of an empty road, her eyes open and as lifeless as she was when she died. I had called out her name as I neared her, and that was when I saw it. So much red.

"It was like a massacre, the blood," I said.

In my dream, I backed away and the blood trickled closer to my feet. I ran when it spilled faster, but it caught up with me, covering up my toes with it. I tried running as fast as I could, my feet splashing the blood all over until I tripped on something and fell straight onto the floor wet with the sticky red ooze. I remember screaming, trying to wipe my face and hands but they were stained with blood, and that was how I woke up; completely wrecked emotionally. Too bad dreams do not come in rated versions like movies. That one would have been totally banned for someone my age. I didn't share all these horrid details with my therapist.

"Did she say anything?"

I shook my head. "No."

"What happened when you woke up?"

"I couldn't breathe properly, my heart was racing… so much was happening at once I had no control over myself," I said. "So, I called Christy."

"And did she help?"

"No, her brother picked up the phone, instead," I told her.

"Her brother?" She skimmed through her note for some seconds. "You've mentioned him a few times in our sessions, and when you do, you refer to him as… evil or the devil's helper, things of that nature. How was that conversation?"

I don't know why it came, a trickle of guilt passing through me and I nodded fervently. I told her he had said some soothing words in a very melodic and calming way, and she seemed to get it because she smiled as she wrote in her note pad. We talked more about my recent damsel in distress situation; of me fainting and being carried to the hospital, about my vocal cords getting back into proper functioning and about my parents. I found it easier to open up this time, telling her about how they made me feel suffocated. Getting it off my chest was a relief.

"Have you ever told them that you feel suffocated?" she asked me after I was done.

"I tried, so many times, but it's like they never hear me," I slouched in my seat. "Happens all the time."

"What would you call your parents feelings towards you, Jacqueline? How would you describe them?"

I stopped toying with a loose thread at the end of my T-shirt.

"You mean if they love me or not?"

"Yes."

"I feel they don't have a choice other than to pay attention to me now," I confessed. "I feel if Sandra were here, I'd have still been the one who received the lesser attention. Frankly, I don't want it anymore. I don't hate them, nor do I know if I really love them, and I think they feel the same about me."

Afterward was the same routine of me driving back home with my Dad and him asking me if I would like ice cream or frozen yogurt, and me declining as always. Mom was not home when we got back, and I exhaled in relief. At least with Dad alone at home, it was bearable. He would only butt into my life to make sure I was not dying of starvation or if the house was on fire. At least he let me be.

I decided to make use of the brief moments of freedom pending the time my mother would be back. The first place

I went was her room. I had to make sure the coast was clear before I unlocked it and snuck in.

I started looking through her coats and dresses this time, searching for a pocket and checking to see if she had pinned it somewhere. I went to her drawers, carefully searching between garments trying not to move things too much as to make her realize things had been moved. Then, I searched behind and between the books on her bookshelf. I checked under the carpet and the bed, already sweating from my labor. Just as I was about to give up, I went to my one last place to search, the powder compact in her makeup bag at the far end of the drawer and I found the key.

"Yes!" I unconsciously clamped my hand over my mouth as I yelled in victory.

I hurried out of the room, thankful that my Dad did not bother to come check up on me. I unlocked Sandra's door and stepped in, locking myself inside. It might look like an act of courage, but trust me, every cell in my body was screaming at me to get out before it was too late. I could not faint twice, well, there has got to be some statistics somewhere that the same thing cannot knock you out of consciousness the second time.

The second task was to find the diary, because it was not among the stack of books on her table. But after a few minutes of rooting around, I was holding the glittering rose-colored book in my hands, afraid to open it and see what was inside. Her messages were confusing, and the dreams, telling me to help her all the time.

Help her do what?

It was at this point that I wished I had told Christy about this. Maybe two heads would be better than one in this case. Also, she was the intelligent one. She could help me read up about this kind of stuff and tell me what needed to be done. It would take a lot of time explaining everything to her on the phone, and with a mental note to make sure to tell her on my next visit to her place, I slowly opened the diary.

The first and second page held the same message, only that it looked like it was fading away. The third page held today's date, and then there was a new message in shakier handwriting than the other; like it was getting harder for her to communicate.

Don't be scared, Jacky, please.

It was similar to the last one, only this time she repeated it; maybe because I had scared her with my hysteria. I scoffed, *humans scaring off ghosts? Well, that's new.* I closed the diary shut, then exhaling, I did the one thing that was left of me in this situation.

"Sandra," I called, my breath shaky. "Sandra, can you hear me?"

There was no response whatsoever. No blowing of the window blinds, no clattering of books on the floor, no breaking of glasses or things floating around in a swirly motion.

Okay, maybe I just might have watched too many movies.

"Sandra," I tried again. "If you can hear me, please, I need to know how and why I should help you. I'm confused here, sis. I'm sorry about last time, I was really scared, but I am not anymore. I just... I'm going to need more than this message."

I felt it, the whisper of a breeze that toyed with my hair. Goosebumps sprouted all over my body, and I was frozen and too afraid to turn. Slowly, I forced my eyes to look behind me, and I held in a scream at the image that faded in, like a hologram to sit on the bed with me.

It did not look the least little bit like my sister.

Chapter 22

He did look very familiar though. I stared back at eyes framed from a body made up of something like smoke and gas, and the face looked very similar to someone who had died years ago.

"Chace?" I called. He disappeared, then I gulped, fear seizing my bones and looked around the room. This was getting to be so much like a scene from a horror movie, except that this was real and I was not an actress.

"Jackie." The voice was as airy as his being when he appeared in front of me. I shook, then composed myself. If I was going to do this. I had to force myself to.

"Where's Sandra?" I asked.

"Is that any way to greet your old friend?" There was a smile as he floated through the air. I watched him, then he perched himself on the bed back to his former position.

"Does it hurt?" I asked him. "From the fire?"

"Oh, no. Not at all, "he said.

That made me truly happy, but there was something that could make me happier; the presence of my sister.

"Thanks for the doll," he said. "That was a very sweet thing for you to do."

I nodded, then asked again, "Where's Sandra?"

"She's in our world," he said. "She can't come for now because she's made too much contact with the outside world."

"Too much contact?"

"Well, there are a few things I'd have to explain," he moved to float in front of me. He was dressed in different clothes from the ones he was buried in and I couldn't help but wonder if they had a selection of clothes over there at the other world.

"Do you have a mall there?" I didn't think before the question spilled from my mouth.

"What?" He made a sound not unlike a giggle. "No, of course not. It's not like earth."

I shrugged. "Is it something like that the place in *Stranger Things*?"

"No, It's different. It's calmer. It's peaceful and trouble-free."

"Now that's a place I'd like to visit." When he gave me an incredulous look, I added, "on weekends and vacations."

Chace sighed. "Sandra did say you grew up to have a dark sense of humor." He made himself comfortable next to me. I was actually tempted to touch him and see if my hand would just pass through him like in movies, but I kept my hands to myself and let him talk.

"Sandra has to wait for her own slot," he said.

"Her slot?"

"Yes. We all have a period of time we can come see our loved ones, and usually there is not supposed to be any physical interaction." he explained.

"So how does that explain the diary and her coming to me in my dreams almost every night?" I asked him.

"That diary was in her hand when she died," he went on. "So, she took it with her, but at the same time, it's here. She gets to write there, but not to reveal secrets. It's a form of communication, but we're limited in how we use it."

"Secrets?"

"We can't speak of some secrets, Jacqueline," he said. "Sandra should know better than to fuel more chaos in this world. And writing in the diary is hard work for her."

"Fuel more chaos?" I was just getting more confused by the minute. "Sandra is a sweet person, or was I guess, what do you mean fuel more chaos?"

"Your sister believes she died an untimely death, and she needs your help," he explained.

"Untimely death?" My blood went cold.

"Yes, your sister believes she was murdered. And she is going to need your help to find out who did it. That's all I can tell you. Time to go," he said and slowly faded away leaving me to wonder if the whole thing was a trick my messed-up head was playing on me.

No sooner had he vanished when I heard the sound of my mother's car pulling into the driveway. I put the diary back where I had found it, stuffed the key deep in the back pocket of my black jeans, and edged out of Sandra's bedroom as quietly as a mouse.

A few minutes later, when my mother came up to check on me, I was laying on my own bed, pretending to read. She knocked softly. "Coming down for dinner? I brought home Chinese food."

"Sure," I said, feigning enthusiasm. *Act as normal as you can considering nothing is normal*, I said to myself.

Chapter 23

I have watched many episodes of the TV show, *Bones*, with my mother.

I had no choice other than to watch along with her, mainly because she was obsessed with it, and she rules the remote. *Bones* or boredom, my two options. In each episode, or most, there were murder cases being investigated and the culprit was caught at the very end. They had all these tools for detecting clues that would lead them on, and eventually, the case would be cracked.

Chace had told me Sandra had sent him to me, and she would be coming after a long while. He told me he needed to give me her message, a message that left me clueless. I was not Bones, I had no tools. So, if Sandra needed my help, it didn't seem possible. I was just a twelve-year-old whose major headache was trying to solve an arithmetic problem for over an hour. I wanted to see my sister, even if it meant being scared out of my mind or questioning my sanity.

***

I was trying to live like a normal person. No easy task with ghosts appearing and diaries sending messages that told me nothing. I couldn't stop thinking about the fact that Sandra thought she was murdered. I mean, how would she know something like that? Were things like that revealed to them or had she felt she was just too young to die? My thoughts were in a maze of confusion, and the only thing loud enough to shake me back to the present was the cheers of the supporters around me as the home team scored a goal. Christy was cheering the loudest, shouting out her brother's name with enough volume to damage my eardrums. I looked out onto the field and realized Eric had scored a touchdown.

I was at the game partly because I had never been to a game before and partly because Christy came over to my place after school and dragged me into her parent's car to drive there. Eric was waving at the crowd. I had very little interest in the game, so I just clapped like a seal. I might have been enjoying the experience more if even half of my mind was on the game. To that end, I tried to watch and be interested as the contest continued. I started to realize that Eric was really good out there on the field, and I had to say, the game was an intense one. He was an odd one, one-part hero, one-part devil. Who was he really?

In the final quarter, Eric faked a pass and ran the ball into the end zone for the final touchdown which was enough to win the game, 21 to 17. The team carried him off the field, then doused him with a barrel of Gatorade.

After the game, Christy wanted me to go back to her house, but I needed to get to the diary. Besides, Eric was insufferable enough without the extra accoutrements of sweat and glory. His head was unlikely to fit through the door.

It had been nearly a week since Chace had appeared to me and I had a gut feeling Sandra was near. Maybe she couldn't come to me the way Chace had but I hoped she would give me another clue. Something I could go all "Bones" on.

"C'mon, Jacqueline!" Christy whined. "Mom will be making a special dinner for Eric. He was so great out there today. I'm so proud of him."

"I'm sure he's proud of him too," I chided, but Christy's face fell, and I felt like a heel. "I'm sorry, it's just that he's pretty mean to me."

"I just wish you liked my brother more. He likes you. That's why he teases you. And he really liked Sandra."

"What?"

"Well, I didn't want to say anything, but Sandra's been… gone for a little while now, so…"

Christy trailed off.

"Spit it out, woman," I pressed her to speak.

"Eric was pretty broken up about Sandra. I know he didn't want anyone to know, but he really liked her. He wanted to take her to the junior prom, but for some reason that didn't work out."

"How do you know?"

"I overheard him talking to one of his friends on the phone one night when he thought I was sleeping. Said he was asking Sandra. But it never happened. Not too long after that… well, you know." Christy looked at her shoes.

No one can just say she died, I thought. *They're all afraid I might break at the sound of the word. Sandra liked Eric, too. What could have happened?*

"Well, why does that excuse him for being a jerk to me?"

"Maybe he's just upset about Sandra and you remind him of her," Christy offered. "Or maybe in a weird way, it makes him feel closer to you, like he's your big brother, too."

"Well, I wish he would just cut it out. I don't need a big brother. I had a big sister and she was the best. I certainly don't remind Eric of her though. I'm nothing like her. She was the pretty one, the smart one, too. I missed getting on those lines when I was born, I guess."

"Jacky, not that it matters, but you're just as smart and pretty as Sandra was. You're just different, but not less than she was."

"No, but I love you for saying so." I gave Christy and hug and headed home. I needed to beat my mother there and have time to check the diary.

***

When I got to the house, no one was there. *Awesome, no disturbances.*

I let myself in and headed straight to Sandra's room. I had the key on me at all times now and I slipped it into the key hole and swung the door wide. The diary was in the same place I'd found it. Stuck between two pillows on Sandra's pristine bed. It had been a few months now, but my mom refused to move anything in the room, and from the looks of things, she came in and dusted every few days, too. If I were a stranger looking at that room, I would think the young lady who occupied it was fastidious and a near perfectionist. It was really too perfect to be a place a teenage girl spent half her time.

I opened the book hoping I would find something new.

Nothing.

I don't know if it was frustration or stress, but I started to weep. First, it was just a trickle of tears I let run unashamedly down my cheeks, but in a matter of minutes, I was hugging the book to my chest and all-out sobbing.

I missed her.

I missed my awesome, beautiful, smart, cool, funny sister. I missed the way her hair smelled when she was just out of a shower. I missed her slightly lopsided smile and her laugh; that laugh. I just wanted to hear it one more time.

All my life I wanted to be like her. I still did. I cried and cried until I was empty. Exhaustion won. I don't think I realized how very, very tired I had been, and without another thought, I lay my head on my sister's pillow, where she had put her head down to sleep every night of my life and dropped into what might be what a coma feels like. I was out, dead to the world, no joke intended.

Chapter 24

What was probably an hour but seemed like a month later, someone was shaking me, hard, and there was a loud voice calling me back from the depths of my sleep. My mother was shaking me awake and yelling as she did.

"Get off her bed! How did you get in here?"

"Wha…? I…" I could not string together a sentence, not a coherent thought. My mother was angry beyond words at my disturbing the sanctuary she was preserving for my sister's memory. I bolted up, jumping to my feet. "I'm sorry, I fell asleep."

"Get out!" she bellowed, and in her anger, didn't see me slip the diary under my shirt. It had been curled up in my arms and I smoothly moved it under the material of my sweatshirt and ran from the room.

I turned to see her smoothing out the bedspread and fluffing the pillows like she was preparing the room for an honored guest.

I hurried to my room and locked my door. I had enough trauma for one night and had no intention of letting my mother or anyone else in for the rest of the evening.

I sat down hard on my bed and stared at my poster of the Jonas brothers, trying to calm myself by looking at their handsome faces. I sang the first few lines of their song, S.O.S., a subliminal message that I needed some real help here.

After a few minutes, a tiny chill ran through my body and I instinctively pulled the diary out from under my shirt where I had been holding close. Without thinking, I flipped open to the page that was empty just hours before.

In shaky handwriting was just one word.

Poison.

Okay, WWBD – What Would Bones Do?

***

I guess my mother was so angry at me for disturbing Sandra's room that she didn't even try to call me down to dinner. My father rapped lightly on my door and asked me if I was hungry. I pretended not to hear him and had my lights off so it would be more believable that I was simply asleep.

In fact, I was under a couple of blankets using my phone's flashlight app to stare at the diary.

Poison.

It had to mean that she thought she'd been poisoned, but by who, and how? I ran the movie of her last few days on earth in my mind. She'd not been feeling well, a small stomach ache, some nausea, nothing to be alarmed about. What about that last day at school or that last night when we were home?

I tried to remember anything she did or said. It was a bit of a blur, but I was 99 percent sure she'd skipped dinner that night saying she wasn't up to eating. We had Chinese take-out again, leftovers from the night before if I was remembering correctly because Dad had gotten more than the usual, knowing mom wouldn't be cooking for a couple of nights. She had a function at the school that would keep her away for dinner that night and so I guess he figured we could all reheat Chinese food when we were hungry. Sandra had only nibbled on an eggroll and ate some of her favorite, General Tso's Chicken. She liked her food very spicy, but her stomach was off, and I was pretty sure she ate just a few bites. By the time mom got home from her school event, Sandra had gone to bed, and I was watching *Riverdale* on Netflix. Mom seized the remote and ironically, switched to Bones reruns. She was either obsessed with crime or in love with the lead actor, David Boreanaz, who played Special Agent Seeley Booth.

The rest of the night had been like any other night. I went to bed soon after my mom got home and was sleeping soundly until the blood-curdling cries of my mother woke me up to find Sandra, well, the way she was. If Sandra had been poisoned, it could have been any number of ways.

Once I was sure my parents were tucked away in their room, I dared to flip open my laptop. I was going to research every kind of poison I could find. Clues. I needed information and clues.

I had no idea there were so many types of poisons, lots of them found in common household products. Cleaning products, bug spray, and some detergents can be toxic. Perfumes, aftershaves, soaps, and toothpaste, even hairsprays and hair styling products and things you use to care for your cat, like flea sprays and shampoos can be poisonous.

I was starting to freak out at the endless possibilities. How would I narrow this down without knowing what she might have eaten at school that day or even that week? Some poisons take a day or two to work their way into your system.

I was even more shocked to find out some of the things that could kill you in the foods we eat. Pesticides sprayed on our fruits and veggies were on our plates every day and don't get me started on meat. I was seriously considering never eating again.

My stomach was churning, not only from the day's events but from all my unpleasant research.

I decided to put the laptop away do the one thing that would calm me down. I picked up my cell phone and dialed Christy. It was time to come clean. I needed to tell my best friend what was happening in my disturbing life, and I was going to need her help. After all, what would Dr. Temperance "Bones" Brennan do without Special Agent Booth? In this scenario, it looked like I was going to have to be Bones and I needed my "special agent" by my side.

The phone rang and she picked it up on the second ring.

"Jacky! You okay?" she asked.

"Christy, I've got some things to tell you. Better get snuggled in under the covers and you might want to grab your best stuffed animal to hold on to. Things are about to get weird."

Chapter 25

"So, you're telling me you saw an actual ghost?"

"Not just saw him, had a nice little chat with him. You think I'm nuts now, right?"

"Well, it's a possibility. And the diary is writing to you?" Christy sounded more and more dubious.

"No, Sandra is writing to me, in the diary, from the other side. She... oh, this is ridiculous. Can I just come over? I need to show you the diary. And there's a lot more to it all."

"Of course. My parents went to a late movie but Eric's in his room. You'll have to be very quiet. I'll meet you at the front door in 5."

I snuck down the stairs, backpack over my shoulder but the diary tucked in the back of my pants in case I was caught. I figured my mother would look in my bag but hoped she wouldn't go as far as to frisk me. *Frisk me?* I have been watching too much *Bones*. I was starting to think in murder mystery speak.

I made it to the door and carefully opened the front latch, slipping out of the house into the velvety darkness outside. *Safe!* I jogged the three blocks to Christie's house, the moon lighting the way like an old pal. I had to force myself to not look over my shoulder for people, live or dead. It was about 10:30 when I got to Christie's. I hoped I could get up to her room unheard and unseen before her parents, or God forbid, Eric saw me. I needed Christie's undivided attention. I felt so badly about not telling her so much of what was going on for so long. I was anxious to get it all off my chest and I needed her help and support at this point. There was no one else to turn to.

Christy was at the door which she had cracked opened just enough to watch for me.

"Hi," she said in a stage whisper. "Get in here fast, my folks should be home pretty soon."

She pried the door open just wide enough for me to slide in sideways, and as I entered the foyer, we heard Eric's bedroom door open and his heavy footsteps headed toward the landing to the stairs.

Wordlessly, Christy shoved me into the living room and turned to the steps to greet her brother.

"What are you doing up?" she asked.

"I could ask you the same thing," he replied sharply.

"Oh, I was just checking to see if Mom and Dad were home yet. I thought I heard their car."

"They said they'd be home around 11. You need something?"

"Yeah… uh, a snack." She rubbed her tummy. "I'm hungry."

"Well, I was just going to make a PB and J," he said.

"Wow, that sounds perfect. I'll make us both one," Christy said and hustled Eric into the kitchen. I wanted to tell her what was in white bread, but that wasn't the time to blurt out food warnings. I took my cue and headed silently up to her room, settling myself on her bed to wait for her. Five minutes later, she and Eric came back upstairs.

"Night, sis. Thanks for making the sandwiches," he said cheerily. *Who the heck is this guy?* I nearly spoke aloud covering my mouth before I did.

"Anytime, Eric. Good talk," she replied and entered the room carrying half a PB and J in a napkin. She thrust it at me, and I was about to say no, due to my newfound food knowledge, but my stomach rumbled, and I remembered that I hadn't eaten dinner. I took the half a sandwich and gobbled it down in two giant bites.

"No milk?" I asked, but the peanut butter stuck to the roof of my mouth and it sounded more like, "Mo milg?"

"Sorry. I had to convince him that I was working on slowing down with my eating habits to explain the sandwich let alone milk. I'll get a glass of water from the bathroom sink."

She started to hustle out, but I grabbed her arm.

"Never mind."

I swallowed hard and pulled her down close to me on the bed. "I'm fine and we have a lot of ground to cover."

Over the next hour, I told her everything. How the diary had cleaned out all my words replacing them with messages from Sandra and the great beyond. I admitted to therapy and told her that I was actually starting to like going and was beginning to trust Mrs. Gilbert.

Her parents came home in the middle of my explaining what my therapy sessions were like and we had to stay silent for what seemed an eternity until the voices from her folk's room faded and were replaced by her dad's unbelievably loud snoring.

"How does your mom get any sleep?" I whispered. "It's enough to wake the dead."

"Let's hope not," Christy replied, sneaking her head out from under the blanket tent we had made on her bed. She was pretty freaked out about the idea of ghosts and was worried one might appear in front of her at any moment.

"It's okay." I said, pulling her back under the safe space of the blankets. "I don't think they follow me around. It's not like that. They don't get much time on earth anyway and I don't imagine they waste it on sleepovers. We need to figure some things out, but the most important thing I need from you is a place to hide the diary, at least for a day or two. I can't let my mom get her hands on it right now."

She nodded and gently pulled the covers away from us motioning me to follow her. She went to her closet and opened the door. Without making a sound, she knelt down, pulled a few items from the floor of the closet and lifted the corner of the rug way in the back. There, under the rug was a loose floorboard. She worked her fingernail into a small space in the floor and lifted the board up to reveal a hole big enough for a few items to fit. Christy lifted a small, leathery-looking book from the space.

"My diary," she whispered. "Now you know where to find if anything ever happens to me," said softly.

I knelt down next to her and hugged her hard. "Let's not need that for about a hundred years, okay?" A small tear escaped my left eye and rolled down my cheek.

"Works for me." She replied and placed Sandra's diary beneath hers, replacing the board, rug, and boxes. "Let's get some sleep. I have a feeling tomorrow is going to be a very long day."

Chapter 26

We were abruptly awakened around 6:30 am by the sound of Christy's mother pounding on the bedroom door. She threw the door wide open and yanked the covers off us.

"Christy! Jaqueline! Girls, Jacqueline's parents just called hysterically. They said Jacqueline was missing from her bed this morning. Didn't you tell them she was sleeping over last night? We had no idea she was here, either."

"Sorry, mom…" Christy managed before I could jump in.

"It's all my fault. I was having a nightmare and didn't want to wake my mom. I'll get right home now." I jumped out of bed and into my black jeans and tee. "See you at school, Christy."

I ran the three blocks back home in a fast sprint. When I opened the door, my father was standing there waiting. My mom was nowhere to be seen.

"Hi," I said softly.

"Jacqueline. We need to talk." He was so not happy. He was wearing that face he saved only for really bad talks.

"Okay! Where's mom?"

"She left for work once she knew you weren't lying dead in the streets somewhere."

Over dramatic, much? I thought.

"I was just at Christy's,' I muttered.

"Yeah, well that's obvious… now! Couldn't you have woken us? Christy's mom said you apparently had another nightmare." His voice softened a bit. "You know you can wake me when that happens, right?"

"I know."

"Do you?"

He looked hard at me like he was planning to say something else but had run out of steam. His shoulders slumped and he suddenly looked very old to me. I never really thought about how old my parents were and I guess I didn't think much about how Sandra's death had affected either of them. Standing there I realized how hard this must be for them, too. Losing a child, even if not your own actual child, couldn't be easy.

"I'm sorry, Dad." I don't know what came over me, but I suddenly had the urge to hug him, to have him hug me back, and the next minute I was enveloped in his arms, his big belly in the way. I felt tears welling up again. and before the whole thing could become awkward, I pushed away and headed for the stairs.

"Gotta get ready for school," I said and started up the stairs.

Halfway up, I turned back, and my father was brushing a tear out of his eye. *These waterworks have got to end. Pull it together Jacky,* I said to myself and hurried to dress for school.

The day was pretty uneventful. Christy and I took our lunch outside and found a place to sit and eat out of earshot of the rest of the lunchroom crowd. Sarah and Caramel walked by briefly, but no words were exchanged; instead, they all turned their heads as they passed in an effort to show their grand superiority.

"I think Sarah misses us," Christy said wistfully.

"I don't know. She's in the 'it' crowd now. I miss her, but if hanging out with those phonies makes her happy, have at it."

"I guess. So, what's the plan?"

"Right now, the plan is to keep the diary safe until I figure out the plan. I don't know how we're going to figure out who would have wanted to poison Sandra, but we've got to try. Maybe we should make a list of possible suspects."

"Okay, how about Caramel?" Christy said.

"What motive would she have for wanting to kill Sandra?" I asked, hoping she would have a plausible reason to get Caramel tossed into prison for life.

"None. But if she did it, we might get Sarah's head out of the clouds and get her back to being our friend. I do miss her. Stupid Caramel."

The bell rang indicating lunch was about over.

"Come home with me after school. I have to show my face, but if you're with me, my mom won't make as big a scene," I said.

"Sure," Christy said and gave me a quick hug before heading to her next class.

We dawdled a little after school, hanging around the soccer field to watch the team practice. I was in no rush to go home to the wrath of mom, but eventually, Christy and I strolled slowly home. We'd no sooner gotten in the front door of my house when my mother came roaring down the stairs.

"Where is it?" she yelled angrily as she descended the staircase.

"Where's what?" I replied, trying to sound innocent.

"You know exactly what I mean."

She suddenly realized Christy was standing behind me and that she was acting crazy.

"Christy…"

She was about to say something when dad popped out of the kitchen.

"What's going on?" he asked.

"Jaqueline borrowed something that doesn't belong to her and Christy was just about to leave so Jacky and I can discuss it."

She never called me Jacky and I was taken aback.

"Don't call me that." I said angrily. "And I didn't 'borrow' anything. Christy and I are going upstairs to study if no one has anything else to yell about," I said, hoping my dad would back me up.

My mom was starting to protest when the doorbell rang.

"Who would be ringing the bell in the middle of the afternoon," my mother asked, taken aback by the interruption.

"I'll get it," I said in a sarcastically cheery voice. I turned back to the door and opened it to find a small, thin man in a dark grey suit standing in the doorway. He wore a plain white shirt with a cranberry-colored and grey striped tie, and he was carrying a black leather briefcase.

"Can I help you?" I asked, figuring he was some door-to-door salesman.

"Is this the home of Mr. Ben Lautner?" he asked.

My dad, overhearing his name, came up behind me and said, "I'm Ben Lautner, can I help you?"

"I'm with American Heritage Insurance, Mr. Lautner. We've sent you a couple of emails. Didn't you get those?"

"I may have, but I probably thought you were selling something. Actually, if you're selling insurance, I already have a policy." Dad said.

"Yes, that's why I'm here. There's a matter of $100,000, Mr. Lautner.

"What? How can I owe that much?" Dad asked.

"It's not what you owe, sir, it's what we owe you," he replied. "Your daughter, Sandra Lautner, has passed away, hasn't she?"

We all stood in the hallway mouths wide open like a school of grouper.

"Yes," Dad managed to say finally. "But what does that have to do with owning me $100,000?"

"That's the amount you had her insured for, sir. I came to bring you your check."

Chapter 27

My mother grabbed the newel post for balance. My father ushered the little man into the living room and sat him down on the couch.

"Would you like some coffee or something?" my father asked him.

He seemed a little dazed.

"No, I'm good. With checks this size and with it being such a young person's passing, we like to give clients like yourselves some personal attention."

"Understood."

"Umm, excuse me," I piped up, feeling a sharp elbow in my ribs from Christy indicating I might want to keep my mouth shut, but of course, I didn't. "Why did you ensure your 16-year-old stepdaughter for $100,000?"

"Jacqueline!" my mother shouted. "Don't be rude. Your father has the whole family under the insurance policy."

"It's common practice, really." The insurance guy jumped in.

"Why? Wait! Do you have me insured too?" I asked.

"Well, take for example a situation where a whole family is in their car and there's a terrible accident. If one or some of the family members survive, they would need that insurance money from those that didn't. You see?" he answered pushing his glasses back up on his nose and looking quite satisfied with his wealth of knowledge on family tragedies.

"Makes sense!" Christy said, enthusiastically. "Jaqueline, we need to get going. We have that test to study for, remember?" she all but pushed me to the front door.

"What the... Oh! Yeah!" I caught on finally. "I won't be back tonight. Staying over at Christy's, gotta ace that test." I said, and we made our escape leaving my parents and the insurance guy to their own devices.

When we got out of earshot, Christy pulled me behind a tree so we couldn't be seen from the house.

"That was odd," she said.

"Ya think? My stepdad just got rich from my sister's demise. I hate to say this, but wouldn't that be a terrific motive to poison someone?"

"God, how terrible would it be if your dad was the murderer?"

"As terrible as it gets," I answered. "What now?"

"I guess we go to my house and study for an imaginary test but actually brainstorm our next move."

With that, we hustled to Christy's and spent the rest of the night tossing ideas back and forth, looking up poisons, and mostly upsetting ourselves. We both tossed and turned through the night. I kept expecting my mom to show up to drag me home, but she never even called. I wondered if she knew about the policy and was as surprised as I was. I certainly couldn't ask her or seek her advice. But there was someone I could talk to, and the next day after school, I headed straight to the one person I would not have expected to need.

Mrs. Gilbert was surprised to see me sitting in her waiting room, anxiously tapping my feet. Christy was sitting next to me reading an article in a psychiatry magazine or at least pretending to.

"Jacqueline! You didn't have an appointment for today. My receptionist just called me to let me know you were out here. Are you okay?"

"Not really," I replied. "I could use a little advice. Can my friend and I come in and talk to you for a few minutes?"

"I have about 25 mins before my next appointment. Good enough?"

"We'll be quick," I said. *I hope*, I thought.

After some quick introductions, I told Mrs. Gilbert what had been happening. With a little help from Christy and the sugar rush from the Mountain Dew I drank on the way there, I was able to get her up to speed in about 15 of my 25-minute allotment.

"So, your sister is talking to you through the diary, she has indicated she was poisoned, and your step-father just got a check for $100,000 from an insurance policy he apparently took out on her?"

"That's the gist, yes." I replied, and taking a deep breath, plopped down into one of the colorful chairs I usually sit in for therapy.

"Jaqueline, there's something I want to discuss with you, an alternative possibility to what you think is happening, but it really should be in confidence during one of our regular sessions."

"Anything you have to tell me, Christy can hear. And besides, I don't know how much time I'm going to have to make sense of this. He's got me insured too. What if I'm next?"

At that, Christy gasped.

"Spit it out, Doc. If you think I'm crazy, now would be the time to let me know."

"Well..." she took brief pause as if to gather her thoughts. "I know you believe that the diary is being written in by Sandra, but is it possible that you miss her so much that you're creating a dialogue between you and her?"

"You mean, I'm doing the writing, then wishing or imagining it's actually Sandra?" For a moment I gave the idea some serious thought. "I, I... no. I wish that were true. It would be easier just to be crazy."

I reached into my knapsack and pulled the diary out.

"Look at the handwriting. It's shaky and not at all like mine. And you can see it's gotten weaker. She's struggling to be in our world, just like Chace said. And what about Chace? Are you saying I made that all up?"

"Not exactly. That could have been a very powerful wish-fulfillment dream. You loved him as a child. Seeing him, having him tell you that Sandra is okay in the afterworld, would be very cathartic."

"Just look at the writing." I begged her. "Look at the words."

She opened the book and slowly thumbed through the pages. Most were blank, of course. Just a few words were written in Sandra's ever-shakier handwriting.

"It proves nothing," she said. She lay the book down on the little table between our two usual chairs. She sat down gently in the opposite chair to mine. Christy was sitting across the room, crying softly. I guess the idea that her best friend might be bonkers was too much for her.

She closed the diary and sat it on the table between her and me.

"Listen, Jacqueline. Grief is a strange and powerful thing," she said and began to reach for my hand. Just as she did, a powerful wind blew into the room before our hands could touch. I quickly glanced down at the diary and it was flipping open to a new blank page.

"Look! Look," I said, and stood pointing at the open book. Slowly the words were appearing as we watched. A shaky, unseen hand was etching out the words, "Believe J. All true. Poisoned."

Mrs. Gilbert stared unblinking as the message unfolded. As the last word was complete, she slid off her chair and onto the floor into a crumpled ball and for the second time in my life, someone passed out right in front of me.

Christy jumped into action, despite being in shock herself. She ran out to the ladies' room, got a cold compress, and brought it to where I was sitting rubbing Mrs. Gilbert's wrists. The cool water on her forehead brought her around and shortly, she sat up and was coming back to herself.

She took one very long deep breath and said, "We need to call the police."

***

Detective Hardy was a no-nonsense guy. He arrived at Mrs. Johnson's office in less than 30 minutes. I felt bad that I'd screwed up her schedule and probably hurt some poor depressed person who needed their time at therapy, but there wasn't much choice and Mrs. Gilbert made that abundantly clear.

Hardy listened quietly, making notes in his little spiral notebook with a number 2 pencil. He wore a rumpled brown suit and scuffed black loafers. I could tell he was indulging us, but not enthusiastically. Who could blame him? When I got to the part about Chace coming to talk to me and described how he seemed to be made of smoke or fog, he lifted one eyebrow and stopped writing. For a moment, I thought he was going to speak or maybe just rise and leave the room full of crazy females in the dust, but he just looked back down and continued taking notes. I spoke for at least ten minutes with interjections from both Christy and Mrs. Gilbert. Then, with a sigh, I finished with, "So, that's why we called you."

After a very long minute, he finally spoke.

"Ladies," he said with an air of exasperation, pushing a loose lock of his dull brown hair out of his eyes. "I want to believe in ghosts. Who doesn't? I'd love to go fishing with my grandfather one more time, even if I could see through him or he was a puff of smoke but opening up a murder investigation based on what could more easily be explained by a little mass hysteria is not how we do business here in Fairhope. You gotta give me a little more to go on than some scribbling in a diary."

"But, Detective Hardy, I saw the writing appear in the book with my own two eyes. I'm a well-respected therapist, not prone to rash behavior or wild abandon. I'm telling you, no one was touching the book. It was no magic trick.

Someone is trying to communicate with us from the afterlife or at least some other world. And considering the circumstances, it makes sense that it would be Sandra reaching out to her baby sister for help."

"And what about the insurance money? I don't want my dad to go to jail, even if he isn't my real dad. But you don't think that's fishy?" I asked him.

"I admit, that's an odd coincidence and people do kill for insurance money all the time. Well, not in Fairhope, but in bigger places."

The detective sighed and wrote something in his little notebook. He was pushing forty and the lines in his face said he'd heard more crazy stories in his years on the force than he should have, but this one was a doozy and I was willing to bet the first case of a ghost who wrote notes.

"I'll tell you what we will do," he continued. "We have an obligation to follow up on reports where someone could have been murdered. Even if it's a bit far-fetched. I'm gonna open up a suspicious death case and make some calls, do a little digging. I'll need to talk to your folks, Jaqueline."

I gulped hard. "Yeah, I guess so. But my mom is going to want this diary. She was trying to keep me away from it because she thought it upset me. Maybe she thought I was making the whole thing up," I said and shot a look at Mrs. Gilbert who smiled ruefully back at me.

"I'll take the diary with me. It's evidence in the case. I'll want forensics to have a look at it."

"They won't rip it up do experiments on it, will they?" I asked.

"No. They'll handle it with kid gloves. Well, rubber gloves. But I promise they won't destroy it. I can see it means a lot to you. If Mrs. Gilbert says she witnessed writing appearing in it the same way you did, we should try to find out how. I hate to say, but maybe someone is playing an elaborate trick on you. Would there be anyone that teases you or would want to play a gag on you?" he asked me.

I looked over at Christy and she had her head down. "Well," I said.

"My brother teases her constantly," Christy offered then quickly added, "but he's no magician, believe me. He's never gotten better than passing grades in science and math. He's just a tease and he actually likes Jacqueline and he liked Sandra a lot, too. He couldn't be doing this."

"Well, we're gonna have to talk to him too, at some point. Let me get things going, and for now, just try to relax and let us handle the investigating. Don't try to help. Lots of people think they're helping by digging around or asking questions. Let us do our jobs, okay?" he said.

"Will you have to tell everyone that it was us who called you about this?"

"No, we don't divulge information like that. We just say that we got a tip and are following up."

"I'm pretty sure my folks will know it was me, but thanks for that anyway. Maybe it will take them a minute to figure it out." I replied.

He said his goodbyes and promised to be in touch.

"What now?" I asked, looking back and forth between my best friend and my therapist.

"We wait." Mrs. Gilbert replied.

Chapter 28

Needless to say. I was scared to go home. Even though Detective Hardy said to try to relax and let him handle things, I knew my parents were going to blow their stacks when the police came to question my dad. When I finally slipped in through the front door, I expected a commotion. I was surprised to find my parents in the kitchen preparing dinner. They were alarmingly quiet.

"Hey," I said with a small wave.

"Hello, dear," my father replied. You're home late from school.

"Yeah, I stayed to work on some extra credit for math with Mr. Stanley."

"Did you pass your test?" my mother asked.

"Huh? What test?"

"The one Christy rushed you away to study for," she replied with a suspicious lilt in her voice.

Busted!

"Oh. That got postponed. Our teacher wasn't feeling well. She didn't prepare the test after all."

"Lucky break," mom answered. "Which class?"

Ahh! Think fast, Jacky. "English! Mrs. Wentworth. Good thing, I could use another night to study. Mind if I go back to Christy's after dinner?"

"No, but we're eating soon. Do you need to wash up? You have about 15 minutes," Mom said.

"Yeah, I'll be down in a few," I answered and headed upstairs.

I washed my hands and face and then went to my room with the intention of laying down for a few minutes to clear my head. I was staring at the ceiling when my door slowly opened. I looked up to see my mother slip quietly in and close the door behind her.

"Where is it?" She asked almost in a whisper.

"Where's what?" I tried to sound as confused as possible.

"You know exactly what I mean, Jacqueline. Where is your sister's diary?"

"How should I know?" I asked but couldn't quite look her in the eye. Lying was never my specialty.

"I hid it away from you for your own good. It's making you believe in crazy things. Sandra is dead, Jacky."

"Don't call me that. Only Sandra can call me that." I responded through clenched teeth.

"Sandra can't call you anything anymore, honey," Mom said trying to soften her tone. "She's gone, and as much as we may wish for her to still be here, that's all in your head. You're the only person writing in that diary. I saw the entries. The handwriting is shaky. It's not Sandra's. Hers was meticulous. I want you to get better, Jaqueline."

"It's not my handwriting, mom," I said, and swung my legs off the bed to sit upright. "I swear it."

My mother sighed deeply. "Just give the diary back to me. I'm going to destroy it and end all this. And we need to tell your therapist about all this if you haven't already. I lost one daughter to a grave illness I guess we didn't see she had. Her heart was too weak to survive. But I don't want to lose another one to insanity. That diary is making you insane and affecting all of us."

she said firmly.

"I'm not insane!" I replied. "Far from it. I think you should worry more about why dad has us all insured. Don't you think that's weird? Are you going to take that money? Money gotten from Sandra dying?"

"No matter how I feel about it, I have to understand that your father was looking out for all of us. He was trying to protect us, and we will decide what to do with the money one way or the other. We still have a daughter that will need to go to college, so think about that, will you?" she answered.

"Please return the diary, tonight!" she said and turned to the door. "Dinners ready," she said as she exited.

Dinner was weird. Mom and dad barely talked to each other or to me. We ate our meatloaf and mashed, soft food, so not even the chewing was loud. I ate quickly and excused myself, saying I was going to Christy's. My mother shot me a stoic look that I knew meant, don't come back without that diary. But that was impossible. I didn't have it anymore. Detective Hardy said he would call me and let me know when I could have it back, but it wouldn't be until after forensics had a little time to be sure it wasn't some cheap magic trick book I got on Amazon.

When I got to Christy's, we shot straight up to her room to discuss our next moves.

"I know the detective said to stay out of it, but I can't. We have to do something, Christy."

"We? No. I for one, am going to listen to the man. We need to let the police do their job."

"What if we snoop around just a little? If there's something to be found, we're the most likely people to find it." I said.

"How do you figure that?"

"I live in the house. I can look for clues without getting a search warrant."

"You watch too much *Bones*. I'm cutting you off," Christy laughed. "What are you going to do, snoop on your own father?"

"Yes! What if there are receipts for something that has poison in it? Or maybe he has a gambling problem and needed money? People hide all kinds of things. Oh, I know! We need to follow him," I jumped up and started pacing back and forth.

"Follow him? Where? Where do you think he'll go?"

"I don't know, but if he's in some kind of money trouble he might go someplace that will help us figure this out. Like a race track or… or maybe he's secretly a drug dealer."

"You have lost your mind!" Christy said and gently stopped me in my tracks. She put one hand on each of my shoulders and looked me dead in the eye. "You are my best friend and I know all of this has been super hard on you. If you need me to help you figure all this out, I will, even if it means I have to wear a trench coat and follow your dad. But I think we should be very careful not to muck things up. We're barely even teenagers yet, and even though we're pretty smart, I don't think we have more sense than the police."

"I know, but what we do have is more reason to care. Hardy seems like a good guy, but let's face it, he doesn't really think this is serious," I said. "And we know it's serious, don't we?"

"You're right about that." She removed her hands from my shoulder but kept her green-tinted eyes on mine like she was trying to see into my soul. Finally, she said, "Okay so… what's the plan, Bones?" she sighed and sat down on the bed.

"Get your trench coat ready. Tomorrow we follow dad and do as much snooping as we can."

***

For the next two days, we did whatever we could. I shot home after school hoping to beat my parents, home. I rifled through paperwork, old checkbooks, and bank statements that were stuffed in or on top of my dad's desk.

My dad worked from home a lot. To be honest, I never really fully understood what he did for a living, but it had something to do with accounting and statistics. The second morning after we had reported the case to Detective Hardy, we did something completely crazy. We each played sick and convinced our moms we need to stay home from school. I even faked throwing up a little by stealing a little of the leftover meatloaf in a napkin and tossing it in the toilet while making retching noises.

"Oh, my," my mother said when she saw the mess in the bowl. I was on my knees bowing to the toilet and she helped me up.

"It's okay, Mom. I'm a little better," I said and held my stomach. "I can probably go to school."

"Oh, no! Go right back to bed. I'll check on you later, but I have to go in for at least a few hours."

"Don't rush home on my account," I said weakly. "I'll probably just be sleeping anyway."

"Well, okay. Dad is leaving for work in about an hour. I'll make sure he brings you some tea and saltines. That'll settle your stomach some."

"That would be great, but make sure he doesn't change his plans for me. Tell him to do whatever he was planning today. I'll be fine if I just rest."

She bought the whole thing and left me laying on my bed with a wastebasket on the floor next to me that she placed there just in case. *I am going to be a great actor,* I thought, pleased with myself.

Christy's mom was easier to deal with. All she had to do was say she was getting a migraine and she was left alone to recover.

As soon as her mom went to work, she called me and headed to my house where she waited around back for my signal. My father came into my room to bring me the tea and crackers and apologized for having to leave. I thanked him and asked him to just shut the lights off and not worry about me at all.

The second I heard the front door open, I texted Christy to slip up to where she could see his car pull out of the driveway. She watched from behind our shrubbery, and as soon as he was headed down the street, she texted, *coast is clear*. I ran out the front door and we sprinted to the corner where the little yellow cab was waiting. We jumped in, I pointed to the tail lights of my dad's car two blocks ahead, stopping at the light on Main Street and told the driver what hundreds of actors have said in countless movies and TV shows. "Follow that car!"

Once we were settled in the back seat of the cab, Christy turned to me. "Where did you get the money for the cab?"

"It's the last of my birthday money. I figured it was a worthy cause. Thanks for getting the cab there on time."

"No sweat," she replied. "I called the minute my mom left."

"Hey girls," the driver called back over his shoulder. "How long are we gonna follow this guy?"

"Till he stops. When he does, just pass him and stop half a block away. We'll get out wherever that is. Is that okay?"

"Doesn't matter to me. S'long as you're paying." He drawled. He had a Louisiana accent and he smelled a little like garlic but not in an unpleasant way if that makes any sense. We stayed a block or so behind my dad's car as he drove through the middle of town. We passed the building where his company had offices. I knew he went there for meetings and to see clients a few hours most days of the week, but I had only been there once and that was a long time ago. For all I knew, he didn't even work there anymore.

Sitting in the back seat of that cab, nervously chewing on my thumbnail, it occurred to me that I took a lot for granted. I didn't really know very much about the man that had taken me, my sister, and my mom on and helped support. I didn't know anything about where he worked or the details of what he did to earn the money that put food on our table. I didn't know his favorite color or where he went to college; for that matter if he even went to college. I knew my mother had gone to The University of Alabama because she was always talking about the Crimson Tide. She was pretty proud of that fact.

I was trying to remember if he'd ever talked about his hometown or high school days when his car veered into the entrance to the big state park on the outskirts of town. I told the cab driver to drop back a little so he wouldn't see us. We watched from way behind him as he pulled into a secluded little area where there was a pavilion and some barbeque pits. It was a spot people rented to have little private family gatherings and picnics, even the occasional birthday party or low budget wedding.

We had the driver go just past the turn in and we slipped out of the back seat.

"Can you wait for us here for a few minutes?" I asked politely.

"I'm sorry, girls. You look real nice and all, but what if you're lookin' ta beat me outta da fare?" he said in his thick accent. "One a y'all needs to stay in the car."

"I'll stay," Christy said. "Just go see what he's up to and be careful… and quick." She added.

I ran down the tree-lined path to the little grove where the picnic area was. I could see my father's car parked in the gravel next to the little covered cement structure. As I got closer, I saw that he was sitting with his right side to me on a picnic table, his feet on the attached bench. I hid in the bushes and watched him for a minute. He seemed to be holding something in his hands and his head was bent down like he was looking at whatever it was. I realized it was his phone and he seemed to be texting. Not more than two minutes later, another car pulled in. I watched and was quite surprised to see the insurance man step out of the vehicle and walk toward my dad. He stood to greet the little man with a handshake, and they turned toward me to sit at the table. I panicked at the thought of being caught, so I crouched down and crawled on hands and knees back to the cab.

"Christy, you're not gonna believe who just met up with my dad."

"Where to now, ladies?"

I looked at my best friend and shook my head. "Police headquarters." I replied.

Chapter 29

We waited for two hours to see Detective Hardy. Christy's stomach growled so loudly at one point, the officer at the front desk looked up to see where the noise was coming from.

"I'm sorry," she apologized. "I'm starving."

Eventually, they called us over and said we could go back and talk to Hardy.

"Somehow, I knew you two wouldn't listen to me. So, what'dya dig up?" he asked.

"We just followed my dad to the state park."

"No crime in visiting parks," he said smiling.

"To meet up with the insurance agent that brought him the check for $100,000 a couple of days ago. Don't you think that's odd behavior?"

"Hmmm," he pulled his little book and pencil out of his jacket. "I admit, that's a little crazy, but not illegal. Maybe they had some papers for him to sign and they thought it would be better not to do it at the house. Maybe he thought it would upset you or your mom."

"Okay," I replied. "Why not at his office or a coffee shop?"

"Too public?" he answered. "Maybe he's embarrassed about the money. I imagine he might feel bad making money on your sister dying."

"Can you at least see that it's a little fishy?" Christy chimed in.

"Yeah, I'll check out the insurance guy. Well, seeing as how you made the trip all the way down here, I have something for you." he said.

"What's that?" I asked.

He pulled the diary out of his desk drawer. It was in a thick plastic bag. "Forensics gave it back to me a couple of hours ago. They said there was nothing special about it. I have to tell you, I wanted to wait until I heard from them before I went too far digging into this. I was hoping it was some sort of goofy trick book, but it's not. I'm not saying you should have followed your dad today, but you did, and that is a little suspicious behavior. I guess I better have a chat with him."

"When?" I asked.

"Well, do you girls have a ride home?"

"No. We had a cab, but we let him leave. We spent all I had on this much of the traipsing around."

"Tell you what," he said. I need to grab something to eat. It's lunchtime. How about I drive you girls back to Christy's house by way of Burger King. My treat. Then I'll go by and see if your dad is home, Jaqueline. That way, I know you two are safe and you won't be there when I talk to him. If he is a dangerous guy, I would prefer to keep you two out of it."

We ate Whoppers and fries washed down with ice-filled cokes. Detective Hardy dropped us off at Christy's with a warning to stay put. He promised to let us know if anything came of talking to my dad.

Of course, I did no such thing.

I gave Hardy a 10-minute head start, then casually walked back to my house. My dad's car was in the driveway and the detectives were parked in front in the street. I left Christy laying in bed with a cold compress on her forehead. Her fake migraine had become a real thing. She was stressed from the day's events and needed a break from all my problems.

I entered the house quietly, dropped my knapsack near the front door, and walked into the living room like nothing was wrong.

My father jumped up immediately. "Where have you been? I thought you were asleep in your room," he said.

"I was, but my stomach started to feel a little better, so I walked over to the convenience store to get some fresh air and ginger ale. That always settles my stomach and we're out."

My lying was improving. I almost believed that's where I'd been.

"Hi sir," I said over my father's shoulder and I walked into the living room and straight up to Hardy. "I'm Jacqueline," I said sticking my hand out and giving the detective a quick wink. "Sorry to interrupt your meeting."

He shot me a fast grimace, so I turned to my dad and said, "I'll be in the kitchen. I think I can manage to eat something now."

"Hang on there... Jaqueline, is it?" Hardy said. *Boy, he has a shot at an Oscar, too*, I thought. "I'm Detective Hardy. I was just asking your dad a few questions. Do you feel well enough for me to ask you to stay? I may need to talk to you, as well."

"Of course, Detective," I replied a little too politely and sat across the room from him in one of the big easy chairs my parents usually sat in.

"Now, Mr. Lautner, as I was saying, we've had a report from a person who wishes to remain anonymous at this time, that there could have been some foul play regarding your daughter Sandra's death."

"That's insane, detective. My daughter was ill and apparently had some heart issues that went undetected. She appeared to be having a little stomach bug, but it turned out to be more of a virus that ultimately became fatal. Why would anyone think there was foul play?"

"The tip just said that you recently received a large sum of money from an insurance policy you took out on your daughter a few months before her death."

"Yes, but that was a family policy. It covered me more than anyone, then my wife and a small amount on each of the girls."

For the first time, it hit me that I was on that policy, too. If something happened to me, Dad would be able to claim another $100,000. Probably more if mom died. I shivered visibly and my dad noticed.

"Are you okay, Jacqueline?" he turned to the detective. "Is it necessary for my twelve-year-old daughter to hear all of this?"

"I'm fine dad, just a little cold is all." I had no intention of leaving that room.

Just then, the door opened and in walked my mother. She yelled for my dad right away.

"In here, darling." Dad said, and my mom entered the living room visibly confused at the scene in front of her.

"Honey, this is Detective Hardy."

"Detective? Jacqueline, what did you do now? Please tell me you haven't gotten into another brawl with someone." She said glaring at me.

"No! He's not here for me. He's here to talk to Dad."

"Allow me to explain," Hardy said. "We're inquiring into the circumstances surrounding the death of your daughter Sandra. We got a tip that there could have been foul play involved and we have an obligation to follow-up on matters like this."

"A tip!" my mother looked straight at me, "And who was this *tip*, from?"

She spit the words out angrily.

"I'm not at liberty to say at this time…"

"Jaqueline! Did you have anything to do with this? I mean, I know you hate us, but really. "Is this about the diary?" She turned and asked the detective. "No matter what your tip said, I do not believe Sandra is communicating with Jaqueline from the great beyond by writing in a diary. This is why we have her in therapy." At that, she turned to me. "Where is the diary?"

"I never told you Sandra was writing to me," I said.

"In the hospital, after they gave you the pain killers. You were muttering about Sandra and words in the diary. Why do you think I took it away? I saw what you wrote in there and I put two and two together." She softened her tone. "I know you want her back. Everyone does."

"I didn't write in it. Sandra did." I said.

"Mrs. Lautner," Detective Hardy spoke up. "Trust me, I don't believe in ghosts, but after a little digging, it does seem that your husband took out an insurance policy on Sandra and stood to gain a fair bit of money from her very untimely death. That is something we look at seriously. As for the diary…"

"This is crazy," Dad said. "Jacqueline, where the hell is the diary?"

I might have a great career as an actor ahead of me, but not as a poker player. I inadvertently turned my head spying my knapsack which was near the steps in plain view. My mother caught the look, and my luck, she stood between me and the bag. With one swift motion, she went to it and swept the bag up into her arms. She opened the zipper and pulled the diary out. Luckily, I had tossed out the plastic bag Forensics had put it in, so my mom didn't have that ammunition.

She went to hand it to Hardy, and just as she did, a wild wind came out of nowhere and flung the book onto the coffee table in front of the detective.

I've seen a lot of scary movies for a kid my age. I've read Steven King books and my share of ghost stories, but what happened next took the prize for the scariest thing I have ever seen in my life.

Right in front of us, while we all watched, what looked like the shape of a girl's hand, in particular, my sister's hand, slowly opened the diary. The pages were flipped to the next blank page and one letter at a time appeared.

M u r d e r e d P o i s o n

This time, it was my father who passed out. The detective sat as still as a statue, eyes glued to the book.

After what seemed like an hour, the book closed itself. My mother turned and walked from the room. The detective went to my father and patted him gently on the cheeks.

"Mr. Lautner," he said. "Sir, snap out of it."

Slowly, my dad came to.

"Sir, I'm afraid we're going to have to take you downtown for further questioning."

He looked at me. "I'm gonna need that book," was all he said.

Chapter 30

While the Fairhope police were grilling my father down at the police station, my mother and I were tiptoeing around each other at home. I wanted her to scream at me, accuse me of calling the cops on my father, blame me for the diary, or tell me how I was somehow at fault for everything that had happened.

But she remained silent.

That was nearly as scary as seeing my sister's handwriting in the diary. What was she thinking? Was she upset about seeing what we'd all seen? Was she trying to somehow justify or explain it away? I was starting to worry that it was just too much for her and that she had snapped altogether.

I called Christy. Eric answered her phone again. Ugh!

"She's sleeping, Countess Dracula," he answered.

"Why are you answering her phone?"

"She left it downstairs when she came down to grab a snack. I saw your mug come up on it and I figured I would say hi! Miss me?" he asked tauntingly.

"Just tell her I called, oh prince of darkness. My best to your lord and master, Satan!"

With that, I hung up, satisfied that I'd one-upped him for once.

Now what? I can't call Christy. My dad may be getting arrested and my mom is a zombie sitting in the living room staring at the coffee table. I had a sudden urge to talk to the only other person who knew me as well as Christy. I dialed her number.

"Christy?" Sarah answered on the third ring, just as I was about to give up and click the phone off.

"Hey!"

"Hey," she replied weakly. "Long time no talk."

"Yeah, well."

"Are you okay?" she asked, and just like that, she was the old Sarah, the one I'd known since first grade.

"No, I'm not okay. I don't suppose you could come over for a while?"

"My mom just got home. I could see if she'd give me a ride over. Let me ask her."

I waited, holding the phone in a tight grip. Maybe this was a mistake, but I missed my friend. Right now, I couldn't afford to lose anyone in my life. After a few minutes, she spoke into my ear.

"Be there in 20 minutes. Hold on, okay?"

"Thanks, really," was all I could say.

In less than half an hour, Sarah was at my door. My mom was still sitting in the living room and it was getting kind of dim in there as the sun was starting to dip. My father had not returned yet. Detective Hardy had let him drive to the station in his own car, so I didn't think they would be arresting him, but he'd been down there for a couple of hours already and my mind was filling up with images of my father sitting in a dark room with a tiny white light shining on him, Detective Hardy pacing back and forth asking damning questions while the police captain watched from behind a two-way mirror.

Too many cop shows! Damn you, Bones *and* Law and Order*!*

I was so relieved and grateful to see Sarah at my door. We headed straight up to my room, and for the next thirty minutes, she sat Indian style on my bed and listened silently while I recapped everything she'd missed over the last couple of months. When I finished, she stood up, walked over to me, and gave me a long, tight hug.

Christy called around 5 pm. I would say just before suppertime, but I had no idea if there would be any supper to be had. I told her that she'd missed so much while she was sleeping and that Sarah was at my house. She bristled a little at first when I mentioned Sarah, but then said she would ask her mom if we could come over to eat with them. The answer was yes, as usual.

Christy's mom was the mom everyone wished they had. That's probably why Christy was so darn pleasant and genuinely nice. It didn't explain Eric, though. Maybe he was adopted.

"Mom? You okay?" I asked, taking one step into the living room. "Why don't we turn on a light?"

I took a few more steps and flipped the switch that would turn on the white antique table lamps. The room felt instantly warmer despite the chill in the air surrounding my mother and the prior incidents of the day. My mother didn't answer at first, but the lights seemed to bring her around a little. Maybe it just made things feel more normal.

"Yes," she said in a voice much smaller than I was used to. "I'm fine. Do you need anything?" she asked.

"No, Sarah is here. We're invited to dinner over at Christy's. I'll be there if you need anything. I can be back in five minutes, okay?"

I couldn't imagine what was going through her mind. Her husband was being questioned for the murder of her daughter. This isn't supposed to happen in real life, just TV and movies; made up stories.

"Okay, well…"

I had no words for her, so I grabbed Sarah's hand and pulled us both out the front door, gathering all the momentum I could so I didn't get sucked into the vortex of my mother's pain and confusion. I had to keep moving, had to walk or pace or run until something made sense.

Eric was nowhere to be seen when we arrived at Christy's; one small thing to be grateful for. We asked if we could take our dinner up to Christy's room using the excuse that we had "girl talk" to accomplish. Christy's mom knew that we had had a falling out with Sarah and probably assumed we needed time to bond again and get past whatever had happened that was ruining a very long friendship pact.

We took bowls of steaming hot and spicy chili over homemade cornbread up to Christy's bedroom and closed the door.

The first few minutes were awkward. I knew that Christy wanted to grill Sarah about her newfound clique of friends and Sarah seemed nervous, perhaps waiting for that shoe to drop. Christy had never minced words with either of us, but she seemed to sense that this was not the time for that sort of thing. This was a crisis and we needed to be kind to one another. I needed them to be so, mostly because I needed both of my best friends right now.

After a few minutes of eating in silence except for Christy's "mmm," as she sucked back spoonful after spoonful of the delicious food, Sarah broke the tension.

"I see you're just as delighted over food as ever," she said to Christy.

"Me?" Christy replied. "Pineapple upside down cake demon!" she laughed. "I will just be eating my carrot sticks," she said in a voice remarkably like Sarah's.

At that, we all busted out laughing and it was like no time had passed.

"My dad is down at Police Headquarters," I blurted out. "You had to see it, Christy." And I told her of the day's events after I'd left her.

"Do you think they're arresting him? Could he have really done this terrible thing?

We sat in silence and I knew that my friends were thinking about all the nice things my dad had done for us over the years. The trips to Uncle George's, driving us to the movies on rainy Saturdays, taking us for ice cream and tacos. My dad was the one who helped me with my homework and made me fall in love with numbers and math. He may not have been my bio dad, but he never let me down. How many nights a week did he bring home Chinese food because it was my favorite? *Wait!*

"Chinese food," I said aloud without realizing it.

"You want Chinese food now?" Christy asked. "My mom's amazing chili isn't doing it for you?"

"NO!" I shouted and stood up pacing back and forth from the dresser to the door of Christy's room, kicking aside a pair of socks she'd left on the floor as she'd entered. "We ate Chinese food the night before Sandra died and we were eating leftovers that night because whenever my mom is going to have a couple of nights in a row where she needs to be at her school, dad always buys a whole lot of Chinese food so we can just reheat the leftovers on the second night. I forgot that, but that week, we'd had a lot of Chinese food. Mom had parent-teacher conferences all that week. That's when Sandra started to feel poorly. Maybe my father poisoned the Chinese food before he brought it in the house.

He could have added some slow-moving poison in the car on the way home."

"Then why didn't you get sick or even your mom when she came home and ate some of the leftovers?"

She was right. That didn't make sense. Mom always plated our food for us, but when she wasn't home, Dad let us make our own plates. He wouldn't have been able to know in advance what food Sandra was going to eat or be able to manipulate only her plate.

"Yeah! Not really plausible."

Just then, my cell phone rang. I didn't recognize the number.

"Hello," I said apprehensively.

"Jaqueline? This is Detective Hardy. I wanted to let you know that your dad is on his way home. Are you home?" he said.

"No, I'm at Christy's. So, he's not arrested?"

My friends sat up straight, all ears trying to figure out the conversation from my one side of it.

"No, we don't really have any evidence to go on to hold him at this time, but I wanted to tell you something that may be disturbing. Because of... of what... well that thing that happened today, we're going to have to exhume your sister's body and do an autopsy. One should have been done when she died, but your parents didn't see the point and there was no real sign of foul play."

Hot tears sprang to my cheeks.

"I see. I understand," I said. "Does my mother know?"

"Your father has been told and he knows he's not out of the woods yet. He's telling your mom about the autopsy. I didn't want you to be blindsided by it and I also want you to keep your wits about you. Be careful, and don't hesitate to call me if anything happens, okay?"

"Thank you, Detective Hardy. I will, I promise," I said, and clicked the phone off.

My friends were staring at me mouths agape.

"Well?" Christy asked anxiously.

"My dad is on his way home and my sister is being dug up from her grave."

I sat down Indian style right on the floor in a heap.

Chapter 31

I have always been a bit of insomniac, and some weekend nights, after my folks would go to bed, I would stay up and watch movies on TCM. I've always been partial to the old black and white films. With all that had happened in the last few days, my life reminded me of an old Agatha Christie novel called, *And Then There Were None.* They made the book into a movie in the 1960's and changed the title to *Ten Little Indians.* In the movie, ten people are invited to spend the weekend at a mansion by a Mr. U.N. Owen. They're snowed in which makes it even scarier, and soon they discover that none of them has actually ever met Owen, not even the secretary or the housekeeper and cook, a married couple.

The butler serves dinner and he has a tray that holds ten little Indian figurines. He then plays a tape with a voice that is supposedly Owen and he tells his "guests" that each of them has a scandalous secret involving multiple murders. As expected from the title, one by one, the guests start dying off, and as each one dies, another figurine goes missing from the tray. You start to figure out that the killer is following the old "Ten Little Indians" nursery rhyme and that Owen is not their host but, in reality, one of them. So, one of them is the killer. Who do you trust? How can you turn your back on them? How can you sleep at night?

That was the new normal at my house.

Dad was suspected of killing my sister. My mom wasn't sure that he hadn't, and she suspected I turned him in. Dad wasn't sure if it was me or my mom that went to the police or one of my friends. I didn't trust either of them for a multitude of reasons. There was the whole matter of the insurance and my knowledge of that meeting in the park, which I could not disclose. No one knew who to trust and we had to live under the same roof for several painful days.

They searched our house and property for any kind of poison. In the garage, there were several possibilities; rat poison Dad had used in the attic when some squirrels and vermin set up shop up there, weed killer with toxic ingredients, windshield wiper fluid and antifreeze. In the kitchen, there were chemicals that could kill a moose from drain cleaner to that crap that turns your toilet bowl blue. After the police left, I realized any of us could be dead from the stuff we never think about and any of us could kill each other or ourselves on a daily basis. I vowed to "go green" if I ever ran my own household.

We tiptoed around one another; ate dinner in silence. I caught mom staring long and hard at dad one evening while he seemed to be studying the chili in his bowl like there was going to be a test on the ingredients. I heard them arguing in their room a couple of times late at night. The tension was unbearable.

Finally, Detective Hardy came by to talk to us.

"They're exhuming the body today," he said. My mother shivered visibly, and as for me, my stomach was doing somersaults.

"Okay," Dad said. "What happens now?

"We see what the results are. See if she was indeed poisoned or not."

Outside, I heard the sounds of cars pulling up and doors slamming. Hardy heard it, as well, and went to the window to peer out at the sidewalk in front of our house. I stood to his left and pulled the curtain back a little to sneak a look. A big van was parked out front and a couple of local news crews, complete with cameras, sound techs and the evening anchor, Chad Westerly, were crawling all over our lawn.

"Jesus!" Hardy turned to face us. "Someone must have leaked the story. They're going to want to talk to you. I'll go out and see if I can get them to leave."

Hardy slipped out the front door and we cracked a window so we could hear him speak to Chad.

"Hey, Detective Hardy," Chad Westerly called out as Hardy appeared on our front steps. "We understand there may have been a murder here in Fairhope. Care to elaborate?"

A woman's voice sang out. "Hardy, can you tell the viewers at Channel 10 News what's going on?"

"Okay guys, there's no story here yet. We're in the middle of an investigation and we'd appreciate it if you would stay out of it for now. We'll let you know if anything comes of this."

The commotion continued for a few minutes. Hardy fended off questions and told them that none of us would be making statements. He came inside, but the reporters stayed on our lawn for nearly another hour before finally giving up and heading back to their newsrooms.

Hardy was still there when the last of them pulled away.

"Okay," he said. "I'm glad that's over but be warned: they'll be back. The smartest thing you can do is avoid them. Don't engage," he said and stared right at me.

"Got it!" I replied. "No fraternizing with the enemy."

"Reporters are not the enemy. They're just doing their job. But talking to them could make my job harder. Look, I know this is tough on all of you. I am hopeful this turns into the biggest nothing burger in the world and that we find no trace of any poison or wrongdoing and you can all go back to living your lives."

He said then turned to my dad. "You've told us that you're innocent. I want to believe that and hope that we can prove it. I can't imagine what you're all going through right now, but the good news is that we'll have an answer soon."

With that, he excused himself and left us on our own again to go back to our respective corners; mom on the couch zoned out on *Bones* reruns, Dad at his desk in his office, me curled up on my bed, texting my two besties.

I was doing just that when I heard my mom yell for my dad and me to come to the living room.

"We're on TV, on the 5 o'clock news. That's our house," she said.

Yup! There was Detective Hardy and Chad Westerly in all his anchorman glory, and they were talking about Sandra and how they would be excavating her from her grave to see if indeed she was poisoned by her own father. FREAKING GREAT!

My cell phone was blowing up; calls and texts from my friends and schoolmates. I excused myself and told my mom I was going to Christy's house. She didn't argue, and to be honest, I'm not sure she heard me. I headed straight out the front door without realizing that in front of the house next door, a news van was watching my every move. A guy jumped out in front of me and nearly scared me half to death. For a second, I thought I was being abducted.

"Care to make a statement about your sister's murder?" said the young smarmy reporter.

"Yes," I said, and flipped him the bird. I took off running as fast as I could, cutting through back yards so they couldn't follow me. I got to Christy's in minutes, ran around to the back door and texted her to let me in.

"What the heck?" she said when she saw me. "How did the news guys find out?"

Apparently, her entire family, even Eric, had been in their living room watching the news as well. They all caught the perfectly coifed Chad and saw Hardy's brief interview on our lawn.

"I have no idea, but I needed to get out of there for a little while. It's too much, Christy. I can't take the suspense. I'm scared of my own father and I'm pretty sure my mother knows I'm the one that started all of this, but she can't prove it. Hardy is keeping his mouth shut and I love him for it. I hope he's a good a detective as he is a person."

Chapter 32

I stayed at Christy's for a couple of hours. We watched some mindless YouTube videos of cats doing goofy things and skateboarders doing incredible tricks. We put Sarah on speaker phone and talked to her for a few minutes.

"What are you going to tell people at school tomorrow?" she asked me.

"I'm not going to school tomorrow. Tomorrow is… well D-Day."

"They're doing it tomorrow?"

"Yup. I don't think I can sit in school all day knowing what's going on."

"I should ask my mom if I can stay home with you," Christy offered.

"I could, too," Sarah's voice came over the little phone speaker sharply.

"I love you both for offering and I'm not gonna lie. I would love it if you were both with me tomorrow. I have no idea how I'm gonna keep it together. And being alone with my mom and dad would kill me. We could hide in my room all day, eat pizza, and talk about anything else."

My two best friends asked their moms for permission to sit with me the next day and considering the circumstances, it was a yes from both.

The next morning, Christy and Sarah showed up on my doorstep at 9 am sharp with snacks and sweets to last the entire day. Christy's mom even made us an apple pie from scratch with the understanding it was for my whole family to share, not just to be devoured by us girls. She had gotten up at 5 am to make it and it was still a little warm from the oven. The pie made me cry a little. I wanted Christy's mom to adopt me at that very moment.

Detective Hardy told my parents they would not be allowed to be there when they removed the casket and brought Sandra's remains to the forensics lab. I think they were both relieved to be given that directive.

My mother came up to my room around 12:30 carrying a tray with some sandwiches, cold milk, and 3 wedges of pie. She looked like a ghost herself, her skin pale and her eyes sunk in.

"I thought you girls might be hungry," she said softly.

We'd been eating chips and snickers bars all morning, but nerves were running high and we tucked right into the food.

"Thanks, Mom," I said.

Sarah and Christy chimed in with their mouths full.

"Jacqueline, in all the excitement, we forgot that today is a therapy day for you. I'll cancel the appointment unless you think it would help to go today."

"Can my friends go with?"

"I don't see why not. But they'll have to sit in the waiting room."

"I think I should go."

Later that afternoon, we all piled into my mom's car and took off to see Mrs. Gilbert. My mom sat with my friends in the waiting room and I sat with a very nervous Mrs. Gilbert.

"How are things at home?" she asked.

"Terrible. How are you holding up?"

I wasn't sure which one of us needed therapy more that day, but I knew we had to talk. I hadn't been to see her since the incident that happened right where we were sitting. Had that been just two weeks ago? Things were moving so fast.

"I'm okay. A little shaken, truth be told. I saw the 5 o'clock news last night," she said.

"Yes, it seems like the whole town watches Chad the wonder anchor," I quipped.

"The police questioned me. If this thing goes to trial, I may be called in as a witness. I feel as your therapist you should know that I will have to tell them what I saw. I've been trying to erase it from my mind, but I really can't. I'm very concerned about you, Jacqueline. I'm worried about how all this will affect you long term. I felt like we were making progress. I hope this can all be behind you soon."

She spoke with a genuine kindness in her voice and for the first time, I realized just how much I liked and respected her. She was actually on my side and truly wanted me to get better, get past all the grief and turmoil of Sandra's death.

"They're bringing my sister's body up from her grave today," I managed, swallowing hard.

"That must be an awful thing for you to think about."

"Can we play that game?" I answered suddenly.

"What game?"

"The one where you say a word and I say the first thing that comes to my head."

"Why yes, that's a great idea. Let's start," she replied.

"Life," she said.

"Death."

"Love."

"Friends."

"Forest."

"Trees."

"Night."

"Terrors."

"Mother."

"Hurt."

"Sad."

"Sandra."

"Father."

"Fear," I said, my voice suddenly cracking.

She stopped.

"Why did you stop?" I asked.

"Let's try something else. This may sound a little weird, but take off your shoes and socks, okay?" she requested.

Yeah, that did sound odd, but I was finally trusting her, so I kicked off my sneakers and yanked off my little pink ankle socks. Not every part of my wardrobe was black after all.

"I want you to sit up straight but get comfortable."

I adjusted myself in my seat and sat up straighter and taller.

"Good. Now, I want you to pull your shoulders up toward your ears and hold them there for a count of four."

I did as she asked.

"Now let then drop. Relax, and let them fall completely."

When I did that, I realized that I had been tensing up and pulling my shoulders up somewhat the entire time prior to her instructions.

"Great, don't pull them up again, try to keep them relaxed. Now, I want you to plant your bare feet on the rug. Get the heel and the balls of your feet and even your toes to be as close to the floor as possible."

She watched as I squirmed a little, but soon my feet were planted like little tree roots.

"Great. Close your eyes. Keep your feet planted and your shoulders relaxed, and we're going to breathe in only through your nose as we count to four and fill your chest with air. One, two, three, four."

She commanded and I obeyed.

"Now, out through your nose to a seven count; one, two, three, four, five, six, seven."

By six I was running out of air, but we did that eight times. By the third round I had the hang of it. By the fifth round, I noticed something wonderful happening. I was connecting to my breath and the ground under my feet. I felt like I was more in my body than I had felt in months. We stopped and she told me to open my eyes.

"How do you feel now?" she asked.

"Good. Really good. Why haven't we done that before?" I asked.

"Because you never trusted me enough to listen till now," she responded.

She was right.

"You can do that whenever you feel nervous or anxious or even scared. Cool?"

"Cool."

"I know things are upsetting at home and it's a tense situation, but truthfully, do you really think your father poisoned your sister?"

"I don't know what to think; but I know I can't keep sleeping with one eye open. What if I'm next?"

"You never know what lives in the hearts and minds of others," she replied wistfully.

Just then, I remembered something. I recalled my hiding in the closet while my father fell to his knees at his bedside to beg forgiveness for the last thing he had said to Sandra. I told Mrs. Gilbert about the incident. Described my father's actions and apparent emotional state.

"Sounds like he was sorry for some harsh words, not some heinous act. If he was all alone and reaching out to God and Sandra for forgiveness, wouldn't he have confessed to killing her rather than upsetting her while he was at it?"

"Yeah, that does make sense. I don't want him to be the killer."

"If there even was one. Maybe this will all turn out to be a mistake or some elaborate trick someone is playing on you."

"On us, you mean. You've been dragged into this as well," I reminded her. "You saw the same thing I did. No denying it."

"Detective Hardy came to see me a few days ago. I had nothing more of note to tell him than I already had. He asked a few questions I couldn't answer due to our patient privacy agreement. Besides, I don't know anything more than the fact that I witnessed what appeared to be words writing themselves in that diary in front of my own two eyes."

"I'm sorry for being the worst patient ever," I said.

"Don't flatter yourself. I have far more difficult patients than you."

She laughed. "Look, Jacqueline, you've been through a terrible ordeal, suffered a great loss, and are now in a state of emotional turmoil. No matter how this turns out, I hope we can continue to work together to make some sense of all this and help you become the happiest, most grounded, and emotionally stable version of yourself possible. That little exercise we just did is a way to ground yourself, to stay in your body and not float off into your head. Use it," she said.

"Oh, believe me, I will," I responded.

"Teen years are hard enough under normal circumstances. You got hit by a Mack truck of grief. That was enough to handle but give yourself some credit. Most people dealing with the aftermath you're dealing with wouldn't likely be able to cope. You're one tough kid," she finished.

I am one tough kid, I thought. *I can handle all this.*

"Thanks Doc. I'm sorry I didn't trust you at first or want to come here at all for that matter. Turns out, you're pretty darn cool."

"Right back at ya!" she smiled. "Call me if you need to talk. These next few days are going to be rough. Don't hesitate to reach out."

"I won't, trust me." I said.

When I got out to the waiting area, my mom was pacing back and forth, and my two besties were huddled together doing a crossword puzzle in the back of a magazine. Christy jumped to her feet when she saw me.

"Everything okay?" she asked.

"Yeah," I answered, sincerely meaning it. I felt a little better having talked to Mrs. Gilbert. What was the word she'd used? Grounded. I felt more grounded, like I was more connected to the earth and more in my own body than I'd felt in several days, maybe months.

Chapter 33

We dropped Sarah off at her condo and headed back to the house where a rather big surprise awaited us. Uncle George and Aunt Margaret had come to stay with us. I was so happy and excited to see them and so relieved to have more adults in the house to act as a buffer. The news vans were parked outside the house again, but that was no surprise.

"Mrs. Lautner!" a reporter shouted. "Is it true that your husband is a prime suspect?"

Another of them started to follow us up the pathway to the front door, his cameraman taping as we walked.

"How do you feel about the autopsy?" he asked as we hustled up to the house, not so much as turning toward them.

Suddenly, our front door swung wide open and Uncle George was filling the doorway with his huge presence. He pulled us into the safety of the house and slammed the door shut on the vultures waiting outside.

My mom headed straight upstairs without a word to anyone.

I, on the other hand, ran straight into my Uncle's arms and he lifted me off the ground the way he had since I was little. This time, I didn't care. I was so happy they were here.

"How's my favorite niece?" he asked, my feet off the ground sucked into a big bear hug.

"Better now. I'm so glad you came," I replied.

He lowered his voice and moved his mouth close to my left ear.

"I know this is tough stuff, kiddo, but just hold on. This'll all get fixed soon enough."

"Thanks," I said, choking back tears. Maybe everything would be okay. Maybe we could become a normal family if my Dad turned out to be innocent.

Next, he addressed Christy who was clearly a nervous wreck. She was practically jumping out of her skin to greet him. I knew she was being respectful and waiting her turn to give him her warm welcome. She loved Uncle George nearly as much as I did.

"How is my little Christabel?" he said, pulling her in for her own bear hug.

"Oh! I'm so glad you guys are here," she said.

"Where's Aunt Margaret?" I asked.

"Where do you imagine?"

I ran off straight away to see her, leaving Christy and my Uncle to catch up.

Aunt Margaret was already in the kitchen cooking and baking and it smelled amazing. She'd brought a big pot of her nearly world-famous lamb stew which was warming on the stove and she had popovers in the oven rising and browning to perfection. I couldn't wait to get one on my plate with gobs of butter melting in their soft gooey insides. A peach pie sat on the counter top and she was whipping fresh cream when I stepped into the kitchen.

I gave her a quick hug around the waist, not wanting to stop her in the process of making her fluffy tufts of whipped joy.

"You're a food magician, you know that?" I said.

"No magic in it, child, just experience and know-how. Whenever you're ready to learn, you come up to the campground and I will make you the best cook in the family... besides me, that is."

She laughed and handed me a spoon with a dollop of the whipped cream to taste. "Good enough to eat?" she asked.

"Good enough to take a bath in," I said. "I can't wait for dinner. How soon till it's all ready?"

"Very soon. Any of your friends eating with us?"

"Christy is here. She's entertaining Uncle George with stories about our school's soccer and football teams."

"Well, why don't you go fetch her and set the table?" she said.

"Where's mom?" I asked.

"She's resting. I'll go wake her once the table's set and we're about ready to say grace."

Aunt Margaret always made us each say what we were grateful for before every meal. It was a nice thing to do, but I was worried my parents wouldn't have much to say on that score tonight. I was grateful for my friends and Mrs. Gilberts' guidance at our session that afternoon.

I went into the living room and tore Christy away from "our" favorite uncle. She came reluctantly and we quickly set the table for six.

Aunt Margaret slipped out of the kitchen while we were busy setting down our nicest plates, forks, knives, and the good cloth napkins we used when we had company. Uncle George and Aunt Margaret were family and Christy and I practically lived in one another's houses, but today felt like a day when a few niceties would make things better somehow.

I couldn't shake the fact that, somewhere across town, my sister Sandra was back from the grave and being examined as a possible homicide victim. Moreover, her killer could be the very man who swore to love and protect us when he married our mother; the same guy who sat at the head of the table for dinner every night and would do so tonight.

My mom entered the dining room followed by Aunt Margaret who had gone to wake her for dinner.

"Jacqueline," she muttered in a still sleepy voice. "Go tell you father and uncle that we're going to eat now. We'll get dinner on the table right away."

I left Christy fussing with the glassware and lining up the silver like we were at a fine dining restaurant. I think she needed to keep her hands busy to quell her nerves. I found my dad and uncle in Dad's study. My father was behind his desk and Uncle George sat across from him in the arm chair Dad kept for visitors. I stood outside the door for a minute, unseen by either of them. I could hear the conversation though they spoke in quiet tones. I slid to the left of the door to stay out of sight for just a minute to eavesdrop.

"Of course, I believe you," Uncle George said. "I've known you my whole life. There's not a mean bone in your body."

"Thank you, George. This had been quite the nightmare," Dad replied.

"How could they even suspect you? What brought all this on?" George asked.

"There are a few things I haven't told you…" But my father didn't get to finish. My mother was bellowing for me to hustle them to dinner, so the jig was up. I took two steps away from the door and called for them.

"Dad, Uncle George, dinner." And with that, I stepped into the frame of the doorway and smiled at them. "C'mon guys, Aunt Margaret's feast awaits.

Dinner was nearly normal. My aunt and uncle were lively dinner companions and they acted like nothing horrible or upsetting was happening. My mother was still very quiet though she spoke more than she had in days. Aunt

Margaret kept trying to feed us all second and third helpings. I ate two bowls of stew and three popovers. Christy matched me morsel for delicious morsel.

At one point, I realized I'd barely eaten in the last two weeks since all this had taken a turn to crazy town. Christy may have been stress eating, but it was hard to say. The girl could pack food away like a bear planning for winter. My dad once said that Christy had a hollow leg. I didn't get the joke, so he explained it was an old expression meaning someone who could eat great capacities of food but not seem to gain weight; the joke meaning the food just got stored in the hollow space in her hollow leg. It sure seemed like a possibility tonight for both of us. I ate all that food and then had a huge piece of peach pie smothered in fresh whipped cream. Christy had two.

We all pitched in and had the dining room table and kitchen cleaned up in no time. Christy excused herself and said she needed to get home to do some studying. She called her mom to come get her, just in case the paparazzi were waiting to pounce.

I gave her a huge hug and Uncle George was about to follow suit when she cried out, "Oh! Uncle George, I do so love your hugs, but one of those famous bear snuggles and I might pop. I'm so full I may roll home."

"Want me to get the wheelbarrow and push you to your mom's car?" I asked.

"Ha Ha! Very funny but really, not a bad idea."

She thanked everyone and I walked her to the door. The coast was clear. All the reporters had given up and left for the day. Her mom pulled up and she raced to the car, giving me a wave as she jumped in.

Not two minutes later, the doorbell rang. I thought Cristy must have forgotten something and was being polite because we had company. Normally, she would just walk on in.

"Forget some…" I stopped mid-sentence as I swung the door open to find Sugar on our doorstep, not Christy. "Sugar? What are you doing here?" I asked.

"Can I come in?" she asked. "I need to tell you all something very important or at least it might be important. I wanted to talk to you before I go to the police."

My mother came up behind me in time to hear Sugar's last statement.

"Police?" Mom asked nervously. "Jacqueline, step aside and let Sugar in," she commanded, and I moved to let Sugar into the foyer. "What's this about, Sugar?" Mom continued.

"It's about Sandra. I saw the news last night. I know they're thinking Sandra was murdered."

"Yes, it's difficult to think of, dear. Why don't you join us in the living room?"

My mother ushered Sugar into the living room where my father, uncle, and aunt were sitting chatting. "Why don't you sit down, dear?" Mom said to Sugar.

"No, you don't understand. I know the police suspect Mr. Lautner, but I don't think that's true."

"Of course, it's not true." My uncle piped up.

"I think it's not true because I think I know who poisoned Sandra and why," she said.

Chapter 34

I may not have liked Sugar's name and I certainly didn't like her sister, but I knew that she and Sandra were as close to one another as Christy and I were. Whatever she had to say, I wanted to believe that she'd come to us to be helpful, not hurtful.

"What on earth are you talking about, Sugar?" my mom asked.

"I've been watching the news. I'm so upset about all of this. Sandra was more than my best friend. She was another sister to me."

I wanted to say, 'Yeah, and she was whole lot better a sister than the one you have.' But I was curious as to what this was all about and, for once, kept my big mouth shut. Maybe she was just looking for attention. Sugar was as big a drama queen as Caramel, but what if she knew something that would exonerate my father? That would be a big relief for my entire family.

My father stood and walked over to Sugar.

"Why don't you sit down, dear?" he asked, and ushered her to an arm chair where she slumped to sit. "Tell us what you mean by all this."

Everyone in the room seemed to be holding their breath.

"Well, they've been saying on the news that someone tipped the police off that Sandra might have been murdered. That Chad guy mentioned that a tip came in that Sandra might have been poisoned and he said that Mr. Lautner was a prime suspect."

Truth be told, we'd all stopped watching the news. It was all too much to bear, and with my aunt and uncle's arrival and all of us trying not to think about the autopsy, the last thing we needed was to be upset by the news. The whole town most likely suspected that my dad was a killer, and everyone was aware that Sandra's body was back from the grave and being checked for poison. It was no wonder that the reporters were waiting for us again tonight.

"We've been avoiding the news today," my mother told her. "It's too upsetting for all of us. We're under a great deal of stress here, Sugar, so please, if there's information that you feel would be helpful, we'd like to hear it."

Sugar took a deep breath.

"Sandra and I shared a lot. You guys know that. She was the most loyal friend a person could have."

You're preaching to the choir, I thought.

"We shared a secret that I thought was harmless, at least until all this came out about how she might have been poisoned."

"What secret, Sugar?" asked my dad.

"A crush." she answered.

"On who?" I asked, though I was pretty sure I knew exactly who she meant.

"Eric Edgewood."

"As in, Christy's brother, Eric?" My mother responded. "I would never have guessed that. She never said a word to me."

"Well, that's just it. She wouldn't have because she was that good a friend. Sandra knew that I've liked Eric since we were in the eighth grade. She pretended she had no interest in him, knowing how I felt. But last year, Eric started to hang around us all the time. I thought he was finally noticing me, and I was so excited. But I was wrong. It was Sandra he took an interest in."

"How do you know that?" I asked.

"Because he asked her to the homecoming dance. It's a big deal when you're a star athlete like Eric is. To be his date would have been an honor."

"But Sandra didn't even go to the dance. She stayed home with me that night and watched movies," I said. Suddenly that night was clear as a bell in my mind. We watched old black and white movies till way past midnight. There was a Hitchcock festival on, and they played back-to-back Alfred Hitchcock classics. I was so scared after watching *The Birds* that Sandra let me sleep in her room. The thought that my sister had missed the homecoming dance when she could have been there with Eric and instead hung out with me, made my tears cloud my vision for a moment.

"Yes, I know," said Sugar. "She turned Eric down because of me. She told me to go to the dance and get the nerve up to tell him that I liked him."

"But she liked him back?" I asked.

"Yes. She said it was girl code. She would never date Eric knowing I liked him so much. She wrote Eric a letter and told him she had no such feelings for him, and that he was wasting his time on her and to find someone else. She said he was like a big brother to her and nothing more."

"Did she tell you she liked Eric, Sugar, or are you guessing that she did?" my mom asked.

"She didn't have to tell me. I saw the way she looked at him when he wasn't watching her and when she thought I wasn't paying attention. I kept them apart, I guess, but I didn't mean to. And then Eric started getting mad."

"Mad?" I asked. "What do you mean, mad? Was he mad at you?"

"No! He was mad at Sandra. He had no idea I liked him. Still doesn't, I imagine."

She sighed, and I knew that she still had feelings for him no matter how he'd acted toward her best friend.

"After she sent the letter and didn't go with him to homecoming, he started teasing her."

"Teasing how?" asked my dad.

I could tell him that Eric was a master at teasing. He'd been making my life a living hell for years.

"Just stupid stuff. Tapping her on the shoulder and ducking, giving her hair a tiny tug when he walked by her in the hall. We were studying Shakespeare's *The Taming of the Shrew*, so he started calling her "Kate." He told her she needed to be tamed. He said it in front of his football pals, and they all laughed at her. She was very upset."

"Well, that's rude, but not horrible. What does this all have to do with Sandra's death?" my uncle George weighed in. "Just sounds like a school boy crush."

"When the news anchor said that Sandra might have been poisoned, something was niggling at the back of my mind. And then this evening, I was at the Dairy Barn and someone ordered a chocolate malt and it hit me. You know how Sandra loved a chocolate malt?" she asked.

"Of course; she had one every time we went to get ice cream," I answered.

"Well, I remembered the day before Sandra died that we went after school to the Dairy Barn. We were sitting out on the picnic benches with our ice cream. I had a hot fudge sundae and she had her malt. Eric and his pals were hanging around in their letter jackets trying to act cool. I'm ashamed to admit it now, but I was still crushing on him pretty hard and I was trying to act cool, too. Sandra got up to use the rest room and Eric came right over. I got kind of excited, thinking he might have waited for her to leave so he could talk to me."

Why do girls act like this, I thought. *Lord, I hope I never get this desperate.*

"He was all sweet and asked me if I was enjoying my sundae. Then he sort of shouted, 'Look at that there,' and pointed over my shoulder. I turned on instinct and craned my neck to see what he was talking about that made him shout like that, but nothing out of the ordinary seemed to be happening behind me. When I turned back around, Eric was stirring Sandra's malt."

"That's odd," I said. "Are you saying what I think you're saying?"

"What if, while I turned my head for those two seconds, he put poison in her malt?" she asked. "She was complaining about her stomach the next morning and she died two nights later."

"That's pretty far-fetched," my father said.

"Yes, it is," my mother replied. "But what if there's something to it? What if Eric is one of those kids that flies under the radar and is secretly a very disturbed person?"

"Jaqueline." She turned to me. "Aren't you always complaining about Eric? Isn't he rather mean to you, calling you names and teasing you terribly?"

My head started to spin. I remembered all the times Eric had said mean things to me, the time he put chocolate in front of Christy's room to make me think I'd stepped in dog poop. I remembered him answering Christy's phone and singing to me, which at the time seemed sweet, and now, in hindsight, could be a little psychotic.

Eric was my best friend's brother, and she loved him. How would I tell her that we think he could have poisoned my sister because he had an unrequited crush on her? What would I say? Oh, hey, your brother might be a psychotic madman? How do I say, we have to tell Detective Hardy about this and now your family is going to be the one Chad Westerly will be ruining on the evening news?

I don't know if it was all the food, the thought of my sister's body laying in a lab somewhere being tested for poisons, or the idea that I would have to tell my best friend the worst news of her life, but everything in the room started to turn bright white, and for the second time in my life, I passed out cold, this time landing right in my mother's waiting arms.

Chapter 35

When I came to, I was laying on the couch and there was a cold compress on my forehead. My Aunt Margaret was kneeling behind me rubbing my shoulders gently and my mother was perched next to me rubbing my wrists.

Everyone else was standing nearby waiting for me to come out of it. I was only out for a minute or two according to my Uncle George who was the first to speak.

"Oh, thank God," he said, when I opened my eyes. "You had us scared there for a couple of minutes."

"What happened?" I asked.

"You fainted, but who could blame you? he replied.

I slowly sat up. My head was still a little woozy and it felt like a wad of cotton candy was trying to suffocate my brain.

"Don't try to move too quickly," Aunt Margaret said. "You're gonna be fine, though. Just a lot of stress for one day and at your age."

"I'm not as young as I used to be," I retorted. "I feel about ninety, these days."

My mother moved to let me swing my legs off the sofa and get to a sitting position. She scooted over and sat next to me.

"Well, that was fun. What now?" I asked the room with no one person in particular in mind to answer that daunting question. That might have required the whole lot of us to decide a path.

"I think I need to go to the police and tell them," Sugar answered first. "I didn't want to do that until I told you first, but it's important information."

"What about Christy and her family?" I asked. "Should we warn them? Should we confront Eric on our own?"

"No!" my mother said in a loud, firm voice. "Suppose he is guilty? He might hurt someone else. We need to tell Detective Hardy about this and keep quiet until he tells us what to do. They might want to pick Eric up and keep him until things check out at least."

"They didn't keep me. Why would they keep Eric? Just as little evidence here, just a young girl seeing something she's not really sure about and a supposed love entanglement that didn't happen," said Dad.

"Well, at least one of us should go with Sugar to tell him and see what he thinks will happen," Mom responded.

"Why not call him and ask him to come here?" I suggested.

"That might be best. Let's call him and see if he can come right over. He should have news about Sandra soon, anyway. I mean, how long can the testing take?" my mother suggested.

"I'll call him," I said, and as soon as the words came out of my mouth, I realized I had slipped up.

"Why do you have his number in your phone?" my mother asked, with a sharpness in her voice that told me she knew exactly why and that I had blown my cover.

"He gave it to me in case I was nervous and needed to talk to him or in case anything came up that would help the case."

"And just when did he give you that?" she probed.

"That's not important right now, right now we need to get him to come over," I said and pulled his number up, punching the keys to dial him and get off the immediate hook I'd put myself on.

It rang twice and he picked up.

"Hi, Detective Hardy," I said. "There's something you need to know about. Can you come to the house? We need to share some information that might be important, and we need your advice on what to do."

He told me he would be over in 15 minutes and hung up.

"He's on his way. I need to use the restroom." I said and hustled upstairs to avoid confrontation and kill time until Hardy arrived. I dawdled as much as I could without giving my mother the excuse to follow me upstairs and trap me into telling her that it was me who started this whole mess. I knew she knew, and she knew that I knew she knew, but with all that was going on, we'd been tiptoeing around one another. When all this was over, we would no doubt come head to head on it. I was hoping the end result would be worth all that and she would come to see that. I went back downstairs. My mother and Sugar were discussing Sandra's last couple of days. How she had seemed at school and if she'd said anything odd to Sandra.

Sandra was crying a little and she was having a hard time answering my mom. All she knew was that her best friend had been ill, and she felt guilty for not seeing that something bad may have happened and at the hands of a boy she'd had feelings for since she was my age. I nearly felt sorry for her; nearly. She was the older sister of my worst enemy at school, worse even than Eric. Carmel had taken Sarah away from us and was always causing trouble. Sugar was the older version, even if she was a little nicer.

If all of this came out, and it looked like that was inevitable, Christy would think I was siding with the sweet tooth sisters over her. What choice did I have in all of this? Sugar had to tell Hardy and we were dragged into it now. No turning back.

Detective Hardy showed up 14 minutes after my call to him, ever the punctual one. I was glad to see him, even though it was going to mean a big upheaval if he thought he needed to consider Eric as a suspect.

He sat quietly on the edge of his seat in an armchair in our living room making notes in his little book with his usual number two pencil. He nodded his head and looked up at Sugar occasionally in a way that made me think he was summing her up for her level of honesty and the validity in what she was spouting. She spoke nervously and rapidly retold everything we had just heard, barely stopping to breathe, like she had to get it all out quickly or burst.

After she finished, Hardy sat still for several seconds and seemed to be gathering his thoughts before he spoke. Finally, he stretched his legs out a little and straightened up in his seat.

"Well, that is interesting and somewhat upsetting information," he said when he finally spoke. "The number one reason for most homicides is love."

How sad is that, I thought. *How powerful is love that it can make you kill the person that you think you love the most? I don't know how I could kill someone I was supposed to love. That seems more like hate to me.*

As if he read my mind, Hardy said, "They say there's a fine line between love and hate, and I guess it's true. We hear about this kind of thing all the time. We also have a lot of problems with teenagers having mental Illness issues that go undetected. Sometimes drugs are involved. Do any of you suspect that Eric could be using drugs?"

"No!" I answered quickly, but then realized I had no basis to believe anything about Eric and possible drug use. I just knew that Christy would never do such a thing. They lived in the same house, had the same great parents.

"You answered pretty quickly," Hardy said. "What makes you so sure he's clean?"

I told him about how great Christy and her parents were and how they were the nicest family.

"And so, you're close to Eric? You're friends then, and you can vouch for him?" he asked.

Cornered.

"Jacqueline, tell the truth," my mother said. "Tell Detective Hardy how Eric is mean to you and how he plays tricks on you, like with the dog poop."

Man, how I wished I hadn't told my mom about that, but she'd seen the remnants of the chocolate on my shoes that I'd missed when cleaning them at Christy's. She thought I was dragging some sort of dog excrement into the house and I was still angry, so I'd told her about what Eric had done. My stupid big mouth strikes again.

"Dog poop?" Hardy asked incredulously.

"Chocolate, really, but he made me think I was stepping into poop. I guess he thought it was funny."

"Pretty elaborate prank just to make you upset," he replied.

That's it. I've outed Eric as a psycho. Great! Now that the cat's out of the bag, might as well go full tilt.

"And there was that one time he trapped me in his sweat."

"Not following you," Hardy said.

"He was soaked in sweat from football practice and he hugged me and wouldn't let me go so I would stink like him," I answered.

And then Hardy said the words I dreaded but knew were coming.

"I'm afraid we're going to need to talk with him and his family. If he's a danger, we may need to take him into custody."

"I have to tell Christy. I need to warn her this is going to happen," I said.

"No!" Hardy said. "I'm calling in now and I'm going to meet my officers over there. If you call Christy, she will tell him, and he might run." He turned to my parents. "Make sure she doesn't leave your sight. Do not let her call her friend."

He stepped out of the room into the hall and made a call to the station. A few minutes later, he returned to the living room.

"My guys are on their way to the Edgewood home. We're going to take Eric in for questioning and we may bring need to do a psych evaluation on him. This is not going to be easy on his family and I know you're all close." Then he turned to me. "Jacqueline, I am asking you to stay out of this. I get that this is going to hurt your friend, but trust me, it's for the best."

"Yes, Detective Hardy." I agreed, but that was never going to happen.

He left a minute later, and Sugar went home a few minutes afterward. The rest of us sat around the living room in tepid silence. After about ten minutes of tension, Aunt Margaret suggested we all have some tea and she trudged off into the kitchen to make a pot of Earl Grey. A little while later, she returned carrying a tray with a hot pot of tea and some sugar cookies she'd brought from home. The hot tea and sweet cookies made me feel oddly more at ease and I almost forgot for a second that three blocks away, the local police were causing a commotion at my best friend's house. My calm lasted all of five minutes when my cell phone rang. Not surprisingly, it was Christy. I looked down at the image of her trusting little face on my screen and almost didn't answer. I walked out of the room and after three rings, I clicked to accept the call.

"Jacqueline!" she sobbed into the phone. *This is so not good,* I thought. "They took Eric away. Someone told them he might have been involved in Sandra's death. Who would have done that? Eric wouldn't hurt a fly."

As a fly he'd done a little damage to, I couldn't fully agree with that, but I stayed calm and tried to think of how to handle the situation.

"Christy, we need to talk. Will your mom let you come over?" I asked.

"That is a very bad idea." My mother had followed me and was talking in a loud stage whisper.

I muted my phone. "We have to tell her."

My mother shook her head side to side for a no. I shook mine up and down, yes. In the time we argued in pantomime, Christy had hung up.

She was on our doorstep so soon after that, I wondered if she'd teleported.

Chapter 36

Christy was out of breath and sweating. She apparently heard my mother's poor attempt at being soft spoken, and when I didn't say anything for a minute, she knew something was up. She didn't stop to tell her parents she was leaving, but rather just ran out into the night and straight to us.

We got her a cup of tea and sat her down to tell her everything that had transpired. She was tapping her foot anxiously the entire time my parents and I explained what Sugar had said and the outcome.

"Are you telling me that, just because Sugar saw Eric stirring a milkshake, he could be considered a murder suspect?" she railed at us.

"No," my father said. It has more to do with his behavior towards Sandra her last few weeks of her life and the fact that a lot of young people today have problems that aren't revealed until bad things happen. School shootings are rampant. Kids get upset, lose a girlfriend, get kicked off a team, get bullied, and they turn on the whole school."

She looked at me with her big pleading eyes, her tears making the odd green contacts glow eerily.

"Didn't you stand up for him, Jacqueline?" she asked. I looked down at my shoes unable to tell her that I had, because the opposite was true. "What **did** you tell the detective?"

"He asked me if Eric seemed like he could be on drugs or disturbed. I told him I didn't think so, but his constant teasing and thoughtless pranks came up," I said and looked hard at my mother.

"He likes you, that's why he teases you and pranks you. He's weird, but he's not a killer. I can't believe this is happening. I hate Sugar and her awful sister. She has a crush on my brother, and he doesn't like her back. That's why she did this. But you're supposed to be my best friend."

"Now, Christy," Uncle George chimed in. "Jacqueline didn't have a choice. I'm sure they're going to find out that Eric had nothing to do with this."

"You should go back home, Christy. Do your folks know you left the house?" my mother asked.

Christy looked wildly around the room. All eyes were on her and filled with sympathy except mine. Mine were pleading for her to forgive me, to understand what we were all going through and how upset I was to see her hurt. But she finally locked her eyes on mine and there was no forgiveness in them.

"If my brother gets arrested for something he didn't do, I will never forgive you," she said and stormed out into the night.

I ran straight to my room and cried for a very long time.

The next day I had no choice but to face school. I'd missed too many days and there were assignments I needed to catch up on. I knew it was going to be brutal seeing Christy, if she even showed up. I walked straight into Caramel as I closed my locker. She and her pals were standing there waiting for me.

"Your family sure is famous," she drawled. "What's it like to be a household name?"

"What's it like to be the most mean-spirited person in the entire school, possibly the whole town? You might want to check with your sister. I have a feeling she's going to be pretty famous soon, too." I said, and hustled off to class.

Christy was absent.

I tried texting her at lunch which I ate under a tree outside far away from everyone and attempted to reach her every other chance I could. She wasn't answering. The school was buzzing about Eric. I guessed that Sugar had told too many of her friends and rumors had started. After school, I started for the exit when Sarah came up to meet me.

"We need to talk," she said, and pulled me into an abandoned classroom shutting the door behind her. "Caramel is telling everyone that Eric may have killed your sister. What the hell is going on?"

"Oh, duh!" I said. "Of course, Caramel is the one telling people. I was hoping Sugar had the sense to keep her mouth shut like Detective Hardy asked, but of course she told her mean-mouthed little sister."

"So, it's true? Eric may have had something to do with this?" she asked.

"I don't know. All I know is Christy is beside herself, Eric was brought in for questioning, and we don't even know if Sandra was poisoned or this is all some bad dream I'm having."

"I need to talk to Christy, but my parents are watching me like a hawk. The detective told me to stay out of it. They're picking me up from school and I'm not allowed to leave the house."

"I can go," Sarah responded.

"You can? You'd go over and see her?"

"She's my friend, too. Look, I've told you I'm sorry about breaking things off with you guys. Popularity is a seductive thing. But I'm not a terrible person. I know who my real friends are and that's you and Christy. I'll head over there and make her talk to me. Okay?"

I hugged her so hard I nearly knocked the breath out of both of us.

"Thank you. I love you so much. I hope you know that," I said.

"Ditto," she replied.

We planned to talk in an hour. I would go up to my room saying I needed a nap and Sarah would get Christy to talk to me on cell phone if she could get her to. If not, she would call me and update me on what was happening either way.

My father and uncle were in the car waiting for me outside the building. I hopped in quickly, not wanting to talk to anyone else. I could tell that my schoolmates wanted to ask me what was happening, but no one dared approach me during school hours. I was glad for the ride so none of them had the opportunity to try to get my side of things after school.

"Jacqueline, we have some news. It's very upsetting news and in a way good news for your dad, but might not be for your friend's brother," my uncle stated.

"What? What happened?"

"The results of the autopsy came back. Sandra was indeed poisoned," he continued.

"But none of the toxic things around the house are a match," my father said. "It seems they feel I'm not their number one suspect any longer."

I sat back in my chair not knowing what to feel or think. I was relieved that my father was no longer a key suspect. I was hopeful that he would be cleared and that no matter what the reasoning for his oddly-timed insurance purchase was, it had nothing to do with poisoning my sister.

My poor sister. She lay on a table somewhere, at least her body did, and she was actually poisoned. She was right.

Her communication with me had wrought the truth. But now what?

"I'm glad, Dad," I finally managed. "What will happen now?"

"We don't know, but the police apparently still have Eric in custody. Detective Hardy said that they are getting a search warrant to go through his room and the house to see if there's anything to match him up with all of this. They're working to narrow down the exact source of the poison, but they know that it's organic," my father stated.

"Organic?" I asked.

"From some plant base, not a chemical. They should know soon," he replied.

A little less than an hour later, I was pacing in my room waiting for Sarah to call me. I finally heard the tiny ding that said I had a text message. It was from Sarah. "Call me," was the message.

I crawled into my closet and closed the door most of the way, leaving only a crack of an opening so I could see my bedroom door in case anyone came in and called Sarah.

"How is she?" I asked, when she answered.

"She's inconsolable."

"Will she talk to me?"

"No," Sarah replied quickly. "She feels betrayed, but I know she'll come to realize this is in no way your fault. She just needs someone to blame right now. I don't know what to think."

Then she lowered her voice. "She went through Eric's things last night when her folks finally fell asleep. Jacqueline, there were some very unsettling things in his desk drawer."

"Like what?" I asked.

"A letter from your sister saying she wasn't interested in dating him, that he was like a brother. It looked like he'd crumpled it up but then uncrumpled it and folded it. And there were holes in it, like he'd thrown darts at it maybe."

"Sugar told us Sandra had written that to him."

"And there was a poem or maybe song lyrics about a girl breaking his 'vengeful heart.' It was very dark. He was clearly very broken up about Sandra," Sarah said.

"What did she do with the letter and the poem?" I asked.

"She was going to burn them, but she got scared. I made her put them back. If Eric is disturbed and they let him go, he would probably freak out if they were missing. I'm scared, Jacqueline. I don't know what to do or what to think."

Just as Sarah finished speaking, I heard what sounded like a commotion where she was. There was a lot of noise and loud voices.

"What's going on?" I asked.

"I don't know. Let me find out. Call you back in a few," she said and hung up.

I waited for what seemed like hours choosing to sit in the semi-darkness of my closet, knees up against my chest. It felt better to be balled up and to be as small as I could make myself. I felt like the whole world was turning upside down.

Chapter 37

When Sarah finally called back, she was at home. Her mom had come to get her when all hell had broken loose at the Edgewood household. Apparently, the lab had come back with a definitive answer on the poison. Sandra had ingested a mushroom called a Destroying Angel Mushroom. It was a white ball-shaped mushroom and fairly common. I looked it up and the symptoms can take up to a day or two to show up. It was possible that Eric could have dried one, ground it into some sort of power and put into Sandra's milkshake. It was far-fetched though, but his motive was not. The police had gotten a search warrant and were combing the path of trees and thickets that lined the back of Christy's house. They found a patch of the mushrooms growing there within minutes. Then they searched Eric's room and found the letter and the poem.

"But the worst part is his terrarium," Sarah said.

"You mean that tank he keeps his frogs and lizards in?" I asked. "Eric had scared Christy and me one night by taking a lizard out and placing it on the kitchen table while we were trying to eat some ice cream. Christy told him to put it back in his terrarium with the rest of his slimy creatures.

"Yes," she said. "The detective was in his room and Eric had placed the same poisonous mushrooms in the glass tank with his frogs."

"Oh, no!" I said.

"The police politely asked me to vacate. When I left, Christy and her parents were sitting at their kitchen table looking like a bomb had hit them. I feel so bad for all of them, Jaqueline. Eric is in real trouble."

She hesitated, took a deep breath that I could hear over the phone.

"But the fact of the matter is, Eric may have poisoned your sister."

Chapter 38

The next couple of days were a blur. They officially arrested Eric on a charge of premeditated murder. He was 17 years old and could be tried as an adult. His bail was set at $500,000 and there was no way his parents could raise that kind of money, so he was sitting in a jail cell waiting for his trial.

I couldn't go to school. More news people showed up every day. They were outside Christy's house non-stop and the story was on the news on stations all over the state. People were calling us from all over the place. Old school pals of my mothers, distant relatives, curious as to how this all could have happened.

My aunt and uncle stayed for several days, but eventually had to get back to their own lives. Christy was still being silent. She hadn't answered any of my calls and texts. She wasn't talking to Sarah, either.

I spent most of my time alone in my room trying to understand how or why all of this was happening. I went to therapy and talked it out with Mrs. Gilbert, but even she couldn't help. I was inconsolable. The police had Eric and they still had the rose diary. I had no way to communicate with Sandra with the diary in their possession.

I needed to know what she was feeling. Did she feel vindicated now that her killer was supposedly caught?

I wanted to hate Eric. I wanted to believe that he was even more awful than I had always considered him to be. But something wasn't sitting right with me. Maybe it was the fact that in all of this, I'd lost the one person I could always count on. She would never look at me the same way if her brother went to jail for the rest of his life for taking the life of my only precious sister. But that didn't feel like the reason. Eric was a prankster, he was downright evil to me at times, wasn't he? Or was he trying to get my attention because he'd had a crush on my sister? Maybe he felt closer to her when he harassed me. How could someone be such a beloved brother to my best friend in the world and a cold-blooded killer at the same time?

My mother came up to bring me a glass of milk and a ham sandwich. I had hardly eaten since Eric's arrest and she seemed genuinely concerned about me.

"You have to keep up your strength," she said and sat down next to me on my bed after placing the food on my bedside table. "This is going to be tough on everyone but in a day or so, you'll have to go back to school and face people. I have to do the same. It won't be easy, but we can't hide in this house forever."

"I can," I replied. "Christy won't take my calls. Sarah says the whole school is talking about this non-stop. Eric is super popular. No one wants to believe he could have done this. Frankly, neither do I, but the Fairhope police think he did. I don't know how to handle this, Mom."

"You haven't called me 'Mom' in a long time," she said. "We've been pretty far apart, haven't we, all of us? Dad, too."

"Well, we've all been staying out of each other's way a long time, not knowing who to trust," I answered.

"I hope we can put all that behind us now that Eric is behind bars. He must be a much more disturbed person than anyone could have imagined. I'll never forgive him for what he did," she said. "Eat your sandwich," her voice cracking as she spoke. She got up and walked out of my room.

I was sleeping soundly when I my phone alarm went off. It was midnight on the nose when I grabbed it to shut it off. *I didn't set an alarm,* I thought. *That's weird.*

As I set the phone down, my window flew open and a strong breeze raced through my room making me shiver. I flicked on the lamp next to my bed and had gotten up to shut it again when I saw her. She was translucent but her whole figure appeared to me. She looked the same as she ever had except that it was as if she were made of smoke or fog.

"Sandra? It's you, isn't it?" I asked.

I should have been afraid, but I wasn't in the least. I felt a weird kind of peace come over me.

She came very close to me and her voice was as I'd remembered it. She whispered in my ear and then she was gone.

I had to try, so I reached for my phone and texted Christy adding Sarah into the thread.

I typed in, "Sandra was here just now in my room. She spoke to me. It's up to us now."

Ping. A response. It was Christy.

"What did she say?"
"Save Eric. Not guilty."